Codename: Starman

Book 4

Spooky Action at a Distance

Books by Mack Maloney

Codename: Starman *series*
The Kalashnikov Kiss
The Sea of Moons
The God Satellite

Wingman *series*
The Odessa Raid
Battle of the Wingmen
The Jericho Storm

Starhawk *series*
Starhawk
Planet America
The Fourth Empire
Battle at Zero Point
Storm Over Saturn

Chopper Ops *series*
Chopper Ops
Zero Red
Shuttle Down

Strikemasters *series*
Strikemasters
Rogue War
Fulcrum

Storm Birds *series*
Desert Lightning
Thunder from Heaven
The Gathering Storm

**For more information
visit:** www.SpeakingVolumes.us

Codename: Starman

Book 4

Spooky Action at a Distance

Mack Maloney

SPEAKING VOLUMES, LLC
NAPLES, FLORIDA
2025

Spooky Action at a Distance

Copyright © 2025 by Mack Maloney

All rights reserved. No part of this book may be reproduced or transmitted in any form or by any means without written permission.

ISBN 979-8-89022-269-5

For "Pistol Pete" Falconi, Radio's #1 Good Guy

Part One

<u>Spooky Action at a Distance</u>

Chapter One

Demask, Ukraine

The artillery was heavy tonight.

The horizon was lit up by giant blasts stretching from Khortov to Solmensk. The night sky was full of suicide drones, HIMARS missiles and jet fighters, dogfighting amongst the stars. In the distance, an electrical storm was approaching, bolts of lightning coming out of it from every angle.

Out of this cauldron, two Mi-24 Hind gunships appeared. They were coming from the northeast, the same direction as the Russian lines, and flying at just 500 feet. But this attempt at evasion would be unsuccessful. The enemy knew they were coming.

There was little left in the small village of Demask. But as soon as the gunships arrived overhead, merciless anti-aircraft fire erupted from every bombed-out building in town. Undaunted, the Hinds returned the fire as they approached the tallest structure remaining in the devastated village. It was an eight-story concrete building that once housed a CD manufacturing company. It looked as non-descript as any place could be in a land completely wracked by war.

It was hard to believe anything could be flying with so much AA fire filling the skies, but the two copters made it through and began a shaky orbit around the old CD factory. Suddenly one dove to tree-top level and headed for the roof of the building. The brutal stream of opposing fire followed it down. Then gunmen on the roof opened up on it with an orchestra of AK-47 assault weapons.

The helicopter came in for a landing, but everyone involved knew it was a suicide mission; the aircraft was riddled with bullet holes even before it touched down. Its pilots were killed instantly, the big gunship crashing onto the top of the roof with a sickening thud, flames and smoke everywhere. The copter's door flew open, and the surviving soldiers inside fell out to be shot effortlessly by the gunmen on the roof. This scene of carnage and cruelty lasted for about a minute before all the copter troops were dead.

The gunmen on the roof were certain the other copter would turn away—but it didn't. It came in as well. But the cloud of anti-aircraft fire to greet its arrival was nothing like the one that had doomed its partner in crime.

By this time, the gunmen on the roof had exhausted their ammunition. They had nothing to fight back with when the second copter touched down and an elite squad of Spetsnaz special forces piled out and massacred the now-unarmed roof defenders.

That went quick. The Spetsnaz soldiers then stepped on and over the bodies of their fallen countrymen—unlike them, mere conscripts all, dragooned from a Russian prison and used as fodder until the real special forces arrived.

They broke down the door leading off the roof and started descending the stairs. They found more defenders on every floor, but now the momentum was with the raiders. There was a series of small but sharp battles. Blinding explosions, gas grenades, flash grenades, the works. The Spetsnaz troops were experts. It was all very violent, but it was also very fast.

When the team reached the sixth floor, the commander paused and called into his field quarters HQ, which was in a tractor trailer sized vehicle parked just over the horizon in Zmelia, on the very edge of Russian controlled territory.

The Spetsnaz commander had two messages, simple and un-coded.

"The fight is bloody," he reported. "But we are closing in on the fifth floor."

***

Inside the Russian mobile HQ, four Spetsnaz senior officers sat before a crude setup of six TV screens. They were watching the attack live on five of the screens via go-pro cameras worn by the Spetsnaz troops. Five screens were showing the battle in all its intensity. But a sixth TV screen was showing something completely different.

On that screen they could see a young girl, barely dressed and "performing" on a kind of paid chat-bait channel. She was dressed like a schoolgirl and was in the process a slowly stripping off her clothes, all while talking sexy to someone on the other line in English.

Then sounds of a commotion could be heard in the background. The girl tried to ignore it and continue the video sex session, but suddenly there was a great flash and the door behind her blew apart. A cloud of smoke obscured the video for a moment. As it cleared, the Spetsnaz troops burst into the room.

Watching Screen 6 intensely now, the commanders saw the soldiers roughly disconnect the girl from all her electronic devices. They blindfolded and gagged her although she was fighting them all the way. Quickly overwhelmed, they took her out of the room, back up the bloody stairway and up to the roof where the second Hind gunship was waiting.

It took off, the officers in the HQ seeing it all from the team commander's GoPro. Another fusillade of AA fire was unleashed as the gunship departed. Once again, the night sky was filled with explosions and tracer rounds. Some of the Russians were trying to restrain the young girl, others were returning fire out both sides of the helicopter. The pilots gave it full throttle and started to climb.

The copter flew about a block away from the building and was still climbing when it was hit by a rocket propelled grenade head-on. The cockpit exploded and caught fire, immolating the pilots, all the horror captured by the commander's GoPro camera.

The helicopter staggered on for about another minute until the flames became too much. The commander's GoPro was suddenly buffeted by a series of explosions and the scene of the ground rushing up to meet it—and then, nothing. The screen went black, and the audio ceased.

The senior Spetsnaz officers immediately contacted two recon drones loitering in the area and ordered them over the helicopter's crash site. They were desperately looking for any survivors but all they could see was the twisted and torn wreckage of the Hind gunship.

It burned for the rest of the night and the debris was still on fire when the sun came up the next morning.

Chapter Two

Near San Diego

"I really don't think you should do this," Angel whispered in his ear.

Lt. Chris Starr shifted uncomfortably in his seat, adjusting his sunglasses. "It's a paid vacation at a five-star hotel on an island full of spooks and zillionaires. What could go wrong?"

They were sitting in his Jag in the parking lot of the Dana Point Marina, about an hour north of San Diego. Nearby, a ferry was filling up with passengers. Starr held a ticket for its next departure. Way out on the horizon, hazy in the morning sun, they could just barely see the ferry's destination: the island of Santa Catalina.

There was a super-exclusive retreat somewhere over there operated by a company called ASI, for Alphabet Soup Investments. It was allegedly a front for the Pentagon's Strategic Security Office, which was a little-known branch of NSIP—the National Security Intelligence Program—under the direction of the ODNI—the Office of the Director of National Intelligence, the highest intel agency in the land. A true multi-letter, multi-service facility, with intelligence officers from all government branches welcomed, ASI was advertised as the place where America's spies went on R&R.

Starr was twenty-seven, five foot nine, blond, handsome, and trim. On graduating from the U.S. Naval Academy, he'd dreamed of flying jets off aircraft carriers. But when a battery of psych tests showed he possessed about a third more ESP than the average person, he was assigned to the Navy's highly secret Naval Intelligence Law Enforcement section as a special investigator.

The Navy shrinks had discovered he had a rare type of ESP called STPA2—for short-term partially advanced precognitive ability. He didn't see far into the future; instead, he usually saw things just a second or two before they happened, just enough time to dodge a bullet or duck a punch. The Navy called it "pre-cog shrinkage."

Being a little ahead of the game made a difference in his job, whether chasing the bad guys, weapons ablaze, or searching for a critical missing clue. As a side benefit, he also was able to utilize his prefrontal cortex the same way people used their TV remote control. He could put his memories on slow-mo, reverse, fast-forward, or freeze, allowing him to detect things not so evident when they were happening in real-time.

These accoutrements had unquestionably helped him achieve his perfect case-clearing rate. But there were downsides. It wasn't always good to know what was coming; it took some of the spontaneity out of life. But second, under extremely stressful conditions, he could get a kind of psychic migraine, an overload of extra-sensory impulses banging around his skull, all at once.

And when that happened, he sometimes heard dead people.

NILE caught cases that were either too weird or too classified for the Navy's regular NCIS agents. He'd been at it for more than three years, working out of the vast San Diego navy base. In that time, he'd chased everything from gunrunners to ghosts.

While there was never a dull moment in his work week, the last few months had been particularly turbulent. He'd nearly been killed by weapons smugglers in San Diego, then almost again in Northern Ireland by the neo-IRA. He'd been trapped inside one real-life haunted house and then again in a fake one owned and operated by the CIA. He'd been in a plane crash, a car crash, and had a multi-million-dollar racing yacht disintegrate around him in the middle of a monstrous typhoon. He'd seen at least two unexplainable visions, had been mentally assaulted by an elephant, and possibly was abducted by a UFO. And that was what he could remember.

So maybe he needed a little time off.

Angel was stunning.

Strawberry blonde, killer body, killer smile, killer everything. She was among the five top cover models in the world. She routinely made more in a day than Starr did in a year. But they were in love and planning to get married someday. They lived together, but their domestic arrangements were unusual. He lived on the top floor of The Park 12 on Imperial Avenue, close to the navy base. Angel lived next door. Because almost everyone they knew, including their employers, would frown on their cohabitation, Starr had built a secret passageway between his unit and hers. They called it the wormhole.

Angel was more than just the love of his life. She'd actually gone on top-secret missions with him, a perfect partner in crime. And many other times, while he was in the middle of a case and prohibited from any kind of communication, they'd stayed in touch anyway, a felony violation of NILE's security protocol.

The way they did this was with their Tomato Cans, their nickname for a near-obsolete U.S. Navy-issued satellite phone sometimes called an XX-12. It worked off an equally antiquated string of Navy surveillance and communications satellites wandering around up in orbit somewhere. Starr had been issued two of the sat-phones shortly after joining NILE. They were museum pieces even then. When a newer, much more advanced sat-phone became available, no one ever asked Starr for the old ones back. He and Angel had been using them as their private voice link ever since—even though it was a federal offense.

If found out, he would be kicked out of the Navy and maybe sent to jail. They'd come very close to that possibility—twice—in the past two months. Still, they believed it was worth the risk.

Drama aside, though, they loved their life together. She thought his STPA-2 was a hoot. He believed her instincts were beyond extraordinary as well. For this and many other reasons, she knew him better than anyone else. And that's why she was feeling off about this trip.

Something seemed a little bent with the cosmos that morning; something in the air. But why was she the only one feeling it? All around them were happy people, excited about going to the island of zillionaires. The sun was brilliant floating on the water, the air was fresh, the breeze warm and mild.

So, why was she feeling like this?

She took his hand in hers and looked into his bleary eyes. Yes, he needed a rest, physically and mentally. But she'd been with him almost the entirety of his spy career and never once had his bosses given him any extra time off. So why now?

She'd begged him to ask someone higher up the food chain to allow him to take some days off at home instead, under care of his world-famous cover model-girlfriend. But as he told her, the Brass insisted he attend the three-day seminar on Alternative Techniques and Methods of Psychology to Release Case-Induced Stress, which included a buffet breakfast and lunch and a themed dinner every night, followed by an open bar and movies. Put that way, it was hard to argue the point.

So, she pulled out the big guns—though not literally—she was barely a b-cup. She began to undo her blouse, slowly, each button giving up after a bit of a fight. Below was not one of her sexy brassieres, if she was wearing one at all, nor was it her creamy bare chest. Instead, she gave him a peek of something else she had on underneath.

It was a costume. Tight, red and blue with a big "S" on it.

Supergirl . . .

Starr gasped. This was a non-verbal invitation to their favorite boudoir game. He caught his breath and pleaded with her: "Why are you making this so hard for me?"

At that moment, the ferry's whistle let out a mighty blast. She quickly buttoned up. "You're right," she said, finally relenting. "Duty calls and I shouldn't interfere . . ."

He let out a long, slow breath. Angel was beautiful, inside and out. Any time spent with her was special. Time away from her was usually not. It had been that way since the day they met.

But she was right: Duty calls. She kissed him softly. "I'll wear the exact same thing when I pick you up Sunday. I promise . . ."

"I'm counting the hours," he said. "And I'm not kidding . . ." He showed her his unimpressive digital wristwatch. It was already counting backward to the time he was due to return.

"Dollar and a half on Temu," he said proudly.

They climbed out of the Jag, embraced, and then she slid behind the wheel.

"Can I shoot the guns?" she asked innocently.

"Sure," he said, though it was no joke. The Jag had two Office of Naval Intelligence-sanctioned .50 caliber machine guns hidden behind the headlights. "Just restock the ammo, please . . ."

They kissed through the open window, but she caught his collar at the last moment and whispered something else in his ear: "Do you have your Tomato Can?"

He nodded while patting his right-side pants pocket. "Do you have yours?"

She nodded towards her Louis Vuitton bag. "I never leave home without it."

"Remember, according to the office, I'll be able to call you on their secure phone once I get there," he told her. "So, we use these only in a huge, gigantic, monster-sized emergency, OK?"

She gave him a mock salute. "Be careful," she said. "And remember I'll be home all weekend."

He tossed his gig bag over his shoulder and headed for the ferry. She watched as he got on the boat and waited until it pulled away from the dock.

Then she blew him one last kiss and he was gone.

Chapter Three

The ride to Catalina was almost idyllic.

The ocean was like glass. It was warm, but not hot. The sea mist refreshing. But Starr wished almost the entire way that Angel had come with him.

The ferry was about three-quarters full. On arrival, he waited for everyone else to disembark. His itinerary indicated he'd be met at the dock and transported to the ASI facility. He watched as the other passengers were whisked away by fleets of elaborate golf carts. Once the ferry was empty, it turned back to the mainland.

Starr sat alone on a bench next to the dock, feeling like he was in an Alfred Hitchcock movie. Did he get the date wrong? Communication from his superiors on this had been minimal—just a terse instruction to report to ASI on Catalina. He checked his cool watch and confirmed the date. Had he taken the right ferry?

He was tempted to use the Tomato Can to call Angel and check his secure emails, but an odd sound distracted him. Like a million bees heading his way. He turned to see a bright yellow aircraft moving at high speed, hugging the coastline and flying low.

"What the . . .?" he muttered.

His first thought was OH-1, a tiny but speedy utility helicopter. His second thought was a flying car. Actually, it was a little bit of both.

The banana-colored aircraft landed in the parking lot. Its egg-shaped fuselage looked like an OH-1 but half the size. And instead of one big rotor, it had eight smaller rotors on eight arms flailing out like the multi-armed princess Durga. Written on the side: ASI Yellow Cab.

A woman's voice emanated from inside. It wasn't the fake sing-songy tone of a robotic hotel hostess. This was straightforward and military-sounding.

"Welcome, Lieutenant Starr. This is our air taxi. Please climb in for transport to the ASI facility."

Starr looked the aircraft up and down. There was no pilot.

"Do I fly it?" he asked.

"No, Lieutenant," she replied. "I do."

Starr had never been to Catalina; he never had a reason to. But as soon as they were airborne, it was clear this was indeed a playground for the well-moneyed. His ghostly pilot provided a running commentary as they flew over the island.

It wasn't a tropical paradise but more like a high desert, covered with scrub bushes and dirt paths that looked like confused noodles. The pilot explained that few cars were allowed on the island, so people got around in golf carts. Hundreds of bison also dotted the landscape.

Turning out over the water he could see Avalon, a large settlement on the island's Pacific coastline. It featured neat, colorful houses giving it a Mediterranean vibe. Its harbor was home to many yachts of all sizes and price tags and even a couple of cruise ships. From the air, it looked like Monte Carlo.

Returning over land, they approached the island's "Airport in the Sky," a civilian airstrip on a plateau 1,600 feet high with no barriers at either end. Starr imagined landing there in a fixed-wing aircraft would be terrifying. Scattered around the airport he saw places that rented golf carts. Some of them looked like used car lots from the air, that's how many of the diminutive, little buggies he could see.

About two miles north of the airport, the terrain became even more rugged and remote. Catalina was 20 miles long and eight miles wide at its widest, with much of it isolated, but this part looked almost desolate.

Which was interesting because flying over one small valley, Starr spotted a crashed UFO.

The air cab had slowed to about 80 knots as they neared their destination, giving him an unfettered view of the ground below. What he saw was a disc-shaped object, maybe fifty feet across, wedged into an outcrop of rock and sand. Wisps of smoke rose from it, and people in military camouflage had it surrounded. A score of vehicles were also around the site—a real anomaly on the car-unfriendly island. Several banks of high-intensity lights were also on the site.

Was this a movie set? His first reaction was to ask the drone pilot if they filmed a lot of movies on the island.

She replied: "Nearly one hundred films and TV shows have been shot on Catalina—from Cecil B. DeMille's 'King of Kings' to 'Mutiny on the Bounty' to 'Chinatown' to an episode of 'The Walking Dead.'"

"So that was a movie set then?" he asked.

She replied: "I believe it is. You can ask one of your counselors for verification."

Then she added: "We're landing soon. Please make sure your safety belt is fastened properly and watch your head getting out . . ."

They passed over a small horseshoe-shaped harbor with ultra-bright blue water and a forest of pine trees on an overlooking hill. The ASI compound was at the top of this hill, looking like a luxurious, if military-themed resort. A futuristic domed building sat at the center, with eight arms radiating from it like an octopus. At the end of one arm was a giant A-frame log cabin, easily 20,000 square feet or more. It was twenty stories high with a revolving blue light at its apex. It looked like a wooden skyscraper, something you might see at a high-end ski resort, if anywhere.

The air cab set down next to the giant A-frame in a parking lot filled with super-elaborate golf carts, some equipped with small satellite dishes. The automatic pilot bid him a pleasant goodbye, ending with, "Call me anytime." Starr climbed out, and the flying banana lifted off and disappeared.

He walked into the lobby of the monstrous A-frame; it looked like an upscale lodge, complete with a massive fireplace. Giant triangular windows looked down on the harbor, offering a breathtaking view of the Pacific. It was so clear, Starr imagined he could see across to Asia.

A stunning hostess intercepted him near the fireplace and offered to show him to his room. Starr followed, noting that the corridors resembled those of an upscale hotel. His room was 1313, which was fine with him. He and Angel considered 13 their lucky number.

So far, everything resembled a very high-class Hilton. But the room itself was styled in post-modern Hippie. It featured a huge waterbed in the shape of a lily.

There were few chairs, but lots of couches and giant beanbags to sit on. The TV screen seemed bigger than in some movie theaters. And the windows had the same impressive view of the deep blue Pacific.

The room's secure phone was red and well-marked. He was planning to call Angel and let her know he'd arrived safely, but he couldn't get a dial tone on three attempts. This let some air out of his balloon. Then he saw his itinerary pop up on the screen of the room's laptop.

"General attendance: 'Orientation & Evaluation, Room 222 in 10 minutes.'"

That sounded boring. But the message was followed by a long list of activities for the rest of the day, including many that were food centric. Buffet breakfasts around the clock, a Lobster Lunch, Mid-day Madness featuring lots of comfort food and then not one but *three* different themed dinners for the night.

Plus, five open bars open 24 hours a day.

How bad can this be? he thought.

Chapter Four

Starr thought he had just enough time for a quick wash-up before the late morning session began.

But then there came a knock on his door. He answered it to find an extremely attractive girl of about nineteen, dressed in a semi-military style uniform with a mini-skirt and heels and huge tortoise shell eyeglasses, like a sexy librarian would wear. She looked like a movie star, not just because of her cuteness, but because she was made-up like someone about to step in front of a camera, powder-puff skin, eye liner, vivid lipstick.

She introduced herself, but still taken aback, Starr didn't catch her name. She was his guide, here to bring him to the session.

"After you," he said, closing the door behind him. They walked in silence for a few seconds as he tried to use his abilities to rewind and catch her name. But it didn't always work when he wanted it to, and it wasn't working now.

"This is an interesting choice of architecture," he finally said. "A big A-frame, way out here."

"Most people want to know if we comp lift fees," she joked pleasantly. "It *is* a little out of place . . ." She paused, then added, "But aren't we all?"

They took an elevator and found the room on the 18th floor of the massive building, almost near the apex. She explained that the 20th floor contained a penthouse that ran the entire place. Starr recalled the top of the A-frame looked almost like an air traffic control tower, complete with a revolving blue light, a color not often seen in aviation.

On the door of his meeting room was a hand-written sign that read: "Regressive Analysis of Past Unexplainable Trauma in the Workplace." In smaller font, it continued: "Goal: To make this a safe place where intelligence agents from all U.S. agencies can be together and share and heal from their traumatic experiences."

"Is this the place?" Starr said after reading the fine print. "I thought this was some kind of orientation meeting. A meet and greet?"

She shook her head and smiled. "Around here." she said. "This *is* a meet and greet."

There was an odd moment of silence—not awkward, just odd. She seemed almost reluctant to leave.

"Are you going in with me?" he asked her.

She laughed sweetly. "No, that's way above my pay grade, sir."

With that, she gave him a hushed goodbye and flitted away.

The small conference room was modestly furnished, with a dozen chairs in the center. The walls were adorned with abstract art, likely chosen to foster a sense of calm and neutrality. One framed poster of a single flower in the middle of a vast snow-encrusted landscape, had a caption underneath: "Sharing is Healing."

He was the first one to arrive. A woman was sitting behind a desk in the corner. She came out to greet him. Her name was Dr. Jess Foster. In her early forties, she was an attractive blonde with an air of composed professionalism.

"Welcome to our space," she said to Starr, managing to look alluring despite her long white lab coat and Birkenstocks. "Our goal here is to provide a safe place for intelligence agents to get together and share their unusual stories, thus healing from traumatic, unexplainable experiences."

He nodded with a little uncertainty. "Yes, I read that on the door. But I was under the impression this was some sort of orientation."

She smiled. Starr could tell her presence was meant to be reassuring.

"Our philosophy is that this is the perfect way for everyone to get to know each other," she said.

He scanned the room. No snacks; just bottled Avian water. That was it.

He took a seat, the only one in one of the twelve chairs. The other attendees began to trickle in, each carrying an air of unease. Starr thought he recognized a few faces from previous missions, but most were new to him. No one said anything to anybody.

"Everyone please have a seat," Dr. Foster said, ushering them in. "Today is about sharing and understanding. Our way of saying welcome. We're here to support each other and to process what we've been through."

Starr had positioned himself so he could see the entire room. Some of the others did the same, but with more hesitation. Dr. Foster waited until everyone was settled before beginning.

"Thank you all for being here," she started. "The things we've experienced, the things we've seen—they can be difficult to process alone. This is a safe space for us to share and understand that we're not alone."

There was a murmur of agreement, but Starr remained silent, his eyes watchful.

"Who would like to start?" Dr. Foster asked, her gaze sweeping the room.

A man in his late thirties, wearing the standard issue nondescript suit, raised his hand. He introduced himself as Agent Ryan Matthews from the FBI.

"I'll go," Matthews said. He took a deep breath before continuing. "Last year, I was assigned to investigate a series of disappearances in the Appalachian Mountains. It was supposed to be a straightforward case—some nut killing people hiking alone—but what I found was anything but.

"We tracked the disappearances to a remote area, deep in the forest. People said the place was haunted, but of course, we didn't believe them. We had three locals with us to act as paid guides, because this is very thick forest we are talking about.

"We camped close to where the last person to go missing was last seen, as good a starting point as any. But then night fell, and we started to hear voices, but there was no one out there. We had high intensity lights, nightscopes, audio detection equipment. Nothing. Yet we could hear them, like they were right on top of us. Voices, growls, and then shrieks. That's when the locals went off the rails. They seemed compelled to run towards this mayhem. We tried to stop them, but they fought us. All three just disappeared into the woods.

That's when we heard each of them let out one last scream—then there was nothing. Everything quieted down.

"My partner and I armed ourselves and went to look for them using our Night-Scopes. But there was no sign of them. It was like they were plucked out of thin air. But we both saw very weird things on our Night-Scopes . . ."

"Such as," Dr. Foster prompted him.

Matthews almost choked up. "I saw . . . things, shadows of things that moved on their own, shapes that weren't human. The official report says those locals got lost, and they did search that place from the air dozens of times, but they were never seen again. And we never cleared the case."

There was a heavy silence as Matthews finished. Dr. Foster nodded sympathetically.

"Thank you, Ryan. That sounds incredibly traumatic," she said. "Does anyone else have a similar experience they'd like to share?"

A woman next to Starr, Agent Lisa Monroe from the NSA, cleared her throat.

"I have one," she said, her voice trembling slightly. "I was part of a task force investigating reports of an alien encounter in Roswell, New Mexico. Yeah, I know, Roswell, of all places. The only reason we were down there is because some people involved had tip top clearance, or relatives who did. We thought it was a hoax, but the deeper we dug, the more real it became.

"We interviewed locals who had seen lights in the sky, and then some who claimed to have been abducted. Then we had two civilians who we had already interviewed go missing. That tripled the size of our assets, just searching for them.

"One night, while watching live footage from a search and surveillance drone, we saw it—an actual UFO. It hovered for a moment before shooting off at incredible speed. We lost contact with the drone immediately after. The footage was confiscated, the civilians were never found as far as I know, and we were told to drop the case. But I can't forget what I saw."

More agents began to share their stories. Agent Tom Wilson from the DEA spoke about encountering what he could only describe as a werewolf during a drug raid in the swamps of Louisiana. Agent Sarah Chen from the ATF recounted a mission where she saw a ghostly figure walk through a wall in an old federal building. Each story added to the surreal atmosphere, and Starr felt a growing sense of unease descend upon the room.

Finally, it was his turn. He took a deep breath, his mind racing through the countless strange experiences he had endured. He chose one that still haunted him.

"About six months ago, I was protecting a federal witness," he began. "We had a lot of bad actors chasing us and I needed to find a place to do an extraction. We wound up taking cover in an abandoned institution for the criminally insane. As soon as I got in there, I heard . . . voices of the deceased, let's say. We finally got out of it, but while I was there, it affected my duties adversely."

Dr. Foster nodded, her expression grave. "Thank you, Chris. It's important to acknowledge these experiences, no matter how unbelievable they might seem."

As the session progressed, Dr. Foster encouraged the group to discuss how these experiences impacted their day-to-day lives. The conversation shifted from the events themselves to their personal toll.

"I haven't been able to sleep properly since that mission," Matthews admitted. "Every time I close my eyes, I see those shadows. I hear screams."

Monroe nodded in agreement. "I've had to undergo therapy. The nightmares are relentless. Sometimes, I wake up convinced I'm being watched."

Wilson added, "I've become paranoid. Every noise, every shadow—it all feels like a threat. It's exhausting."

Starr listened, feeling a rare sense of camaraderie. He was astonished as well. These agents had faced the same kinds of inexplicable horrors he had. They understood the fear, the uncertainty, the isolation. All this time he thought it was just him.

Dr. Foster leaned forward; her eyes compassionate. "It's important to remember that you're not alone. These experiences, as strange as they are, don't define you. They are just part of your journey. And together, we can find ways to cope and move forward."

With that, she finally brought the meeting to a close.

"Thank you all for sharing today," she told the group. "I hope this session has helped you in some way. Remember, this is a safe space. Now, please enjoy the rest of your weekend. And take it from me, the food here is exquisite."

They got up to leave, but Dr. Foster indicated Starr should stay behind.

Once everyone else had gone, she came close to him and said: "Lieutenant, would you mind if we scheduled just one more test for you?"

Starr heard his stomach growl. "Why me?" he asked her.

"Your STPA-2 is a fascinating ability, but there could be downsides to it," she said. "We'd just like to run one more test to make sure."

Chapter Five

Starr returned to his quarters and resolutely tried to call Angel for the second time. But once again he couldn't get a dial tone on the room's secure phone.

He finally, but reluctantly, gave up. He was about to dial the front desk when the room's laptop beeped to life again.

It was the notice for his extra test. tag-lined: IEP Diagnostic, Lt C. Starr, STPA-2. It was scheduled to start in 10 minutes.

Holy crap, he thought. He'd just witnessed nearly a dozen agents have their own personal Oprah moments—he thought that was going to be the extent of the handwringing.

When does the fun start?

He heard a knock at his door; he opened it to once again find his guide. She looked even more attractive than before.

"Time for your next session, Lieutenant . . ."

He began to apologize and ask her name again, but she beat him to it, as if she was reading his mind. "My name is Kelly Kosmo-Bolo. It's easy to forget."

"Not now it isn't," he told her.

It was a short walk to the next session room. While she explained that this would make him miss the Lobster Lunch, she told him she'd check his schedule to see when the next meal is planned. He thanked her. She giggled, but in an embarrassing way and then retreated.

He walked in to find the therapy room was very dark. Very cool. An aroma of something was in the air. Yet another beautiful interviewer greeted him. Super attractive brunette. Even her lab coat looked sexy.

She was Dr. Marielle Laurie. She explained she was here to ask him a few questions about his special brand of ESP. She had a power point ready and waiting. She highlighted not one test, but four, explaining each one.

"Spectral Auditory Perception Analysis, or SAPA," she began. "This evaluates the subject's ability to perceive auditory stimuli reported to be from deceased individuals. Number two: Post-Mortem Communication Simulation places the subject in scenarios where he must distinguish between real-time communication and potential post-mortem messages.

"Number three is the Ectoplasmic Auditory Verification Experiment which verifies the authenticity of subject's claims of hearing voices of the deceased using advanced audio equipment. And finally, the Afterlife Radio Frequency Assessment evaluates if the subject's ability to hear voices from the deceased correlates with specific radio frequencies or other electromagnetic anomalies."

Starr's eyes went wide. He never thought of his precog intuition as something that could be studied, poked at, examined, explained.

"Do I really have to sit through all those tests?" he asked her.

She nodded sweetly. "You want to get to the bottom of this, don't you?"

Do I? he wondered. He wasn't so sure. There were upsides and downsides to his special abilities. He had no idea how they worked or why he had them, but he felt uneasy about delving into them too deeply.

"But is all this really necessary?" he asked. "I can give you four good reasons why this STPA-2 thing that I have saved my life and the lives of others."

She seemed almost amused. "Four?"

He smiled back. "At least . . ."

She pulled her chair closer to his and said: "Okay, try me . . ."

"I was once being pursued by armed men in a Hummer," he began. "My ESP provided me with a premonition of an RPG being fired at my car. This advance warning allowed me to take evasive action, steering hard left and avoiding the missile, which exploded harmlessly. I think my quick reactions and ability to anticipate the attack saved me from certain death."

She seemed impressed and wrote something down on her clipboard.

"Example number two," he went on. "I was in a confrontation with my superior, Bull Parades. My ESP allowed me to foresee Bull shooting me. Despite being overpowered and thrown around, my premonition of being shot gave me the crucial moment I needed to rush Bull, disarm him temporarily, and eventually use a surgeon's scalpel to defend myself. This foresight saved me from being executed by my traitorous boss."

Again, what seemed like legitimate interest. More scribbling on her clipboard.

"Then, while investigating a place called Hell House," he continued. "My ESP helped navigate the hazardous environment and avoid numerous traps set by the opposition. My ability to anticipate dangers and see moments ahead of time enabled me to maneuver through these potentially deadly setups, ultimately helping me survive and complete the mission."

Lots of scribbling, she was running out of ink.

He told her his fourth example: During a desperate escape attempt from a tsunami, his ESP enabled him to visualize and manipulate recent events in his mind. This mental playback allowed him to find the safest route to find shelter behind solid ground. Though he was eventually hit by the wave, his ability to predict and react to the situation helped him survive the impact and avoid a fatal blow.

She just stared at him for a long moment now, her mouth slightly agog at what she'd just heard.

But then she asked: "But when has your ESP worked against you?"

It was a curveball he should have seen coming. He started blabbering at first but settled down quickly. He had to admit that under extreme stress, his ESP often caused him to experience psychic migraines due to an overload of extra-sensory impulses. This overload can be debilitating, leading to intense pain and confusion, which could hinder his performance during critical moments. The mental strain from these migraines is admittedly a significant drawback to his abilities.

He also had to acknowledge the most disturbing aspect of his ESP was his ability to hear the voices of dead people, especially in old, empty buildings like churches and hospitals. These voices were often morose and overlapping, creating a cacophony that can be overwhelming and distressing. This auditory phenomenon not only distracted him at times but also caused a lot of psychological stress, affecting his focus and mental well-being.

And his ESP did not prevent him from being manipulated by Bull Parades, his traitorous boss who used Starr's abilities against him by feeding him misinformation and setting him up. Despite his pre-cognitive abilities, he was blindsided by Bull's betrayal, showing that his ESP was not infallible and could be circumvented by clever deception.

And finally, he had to admit that at times, his reliance on his ESP has led to overconfidence in dangerous situations. His expectation that he could always anticipate danger might make him less cautious, potentially putting him in more hazardous situations than if he were more skeptical of his abilities. This over-reliance can be a double-edged sword, giving him false security and leading to risky decisions.

He looked around for a glass of water, but none was in sight.

She stared at him for the longest time, making him squirm in his chair. Then she said: "See?"

"I'm not sure," he replied.

"Exactly," she told him, springing up from her chair. "See you tomorrow at 5 AM for the first test. Then we'll just tick them off until we reach five. This will take most of the day I would think. And there are no breaks I'm afraid. It skews the data. So, rest up!"

Starr finally found his way back to his room, intending to call down to the front desk and see if he could arrange for some food or something and then finally call Angel.

But when he got there, he found the Secure Phone wasn't working at all now. After repeated attempts, and even though getting dial tones, he heard no rings, at the front desk or trying to reach Angel.

He was about to go down to the front desk when the room laptop came to life.

It read: "Additional procedure requested for Lt C. Starr. Multi-image Subliminal Random Image Test. Room 1391. Starts in 5 minutes."

The knock came at his door an instant later. It was Kelly Kronos. Same uniform. Same heels. Same glasses. Same smile.

"Time for your next test," she said.

Chapter Six

Five minutes later, Starr was inside a sterile room known as Viewing Cube 6. It was in the subbasement of the huge A-Frame structure, its door painted bright red with a large, can't-miss-it "Restricted" sign tacked on to it.

Inside, the walls were stark white, the only color coming from the various monitors and devices lining the room. A large TV monitor was attached to the wall in front of him. He was sitting in a theater seat that resembled an elaborate recliner. This place was configured for an audience of one.

At the moment, he was a bad mix of anticipation and unease, his stomach growling in 4/4 time. He wished he'd listened to Angel and had recuperated from his last few months at home.

"Ready, Lieutenant Starr?" Dr. Foster asked, her voice calm and professional. She stood at a large console about five feet behind him, her fingers hovering over the controls. "The idea here is that we've taken a number of random images, edited them together so that they'll go by so quickly, they'll only make sense to you on a subliminal level."

"And we are doing this because?" Starr asked.

"It's kind of like testing your ESP reflexes," she explained, but not all that well. "We can measure almost exactly the level of your STPA-2 just by seeing how you react to these random images."

"And we're doing *that* because?"

She cleared her throat. "It's really just a pre-test for the panel of tests we are doing tomorrow. We are starting so early; I thought it's best we get this one out of the way now."

He still didn't understand it, but he was so focused on calling Angel and getting something to eat and drink afterwards, that he just gave her the thumbs up.

"Let's get it over with," he said.

Dr. Foster pressed a button, and the lights dimmed. A large screen in front of Starr flickered to life. It was all static at first, but then began a rapid succession of images. Abstract shapes, random landscapes, bizarre patterns that had no meaning. He could just barely make them out, they were moving so fast.

This went on for almost five minutes . . . but then something unexpected happened. Among the nonsensical visuals, he suddenly saw a fleeting glimpse of a picture that made his heart skip a beat. It was of an antique-looking satellite, about 100 feet long and resembling a giant medieval chalice, with a cup at both ends. In the image, it was up in orbit and pointed directly at the Earth.

Because of his STPA-2, he was able to retain it for a second or two longer than the others whizzing by, long enough to see it clearly.

Knowledge of this bizarre satellite wasn't just top secret, it was deeply, deeply classified stuff. The satellite's ability to observe and collect vast amounts of data was mind-blowing. But it is also equipped with incredibly advanced artificial intelligence, making it capable of performing tasks that seem almost divine. But the fact that it looked like it was built during the Renaissance and that no one knew exactly who built it were the strangest things of all.

Starr became involved when he and a detective from the Irish Government named Maura McCann were tasked with finding out if the satellite was responsible for helping a wayward SEAL chaplain named Father Friendly win millions of dollars at a casino by manipulating the electronic systems of the games he played. But when they stumbled upon the place where the satellite was under constant watch and scrutiny—an observatory in Arizona that was owned by the Vatican—they had their memories washed. They remembered going into the place, but they couldn't remember much of what happened inside.

But why would the ASI people show this to him now? The only person who could verify what happened to them was Maura McCann—and he was sure she was nowhere near this place.

He forced himself to take deep, steady breaths, his eyes darting from one random image to the next, wondering if he'd see it again. Sure enough, the nonsensical scenes started being repeated: swirling colors, strange symbols, abstract doodling. But then the ancient satellite came back again and again – and again. Clearer, brighter, seemingly lasting a bit longer each time, he felt himself jump every time it appeared.

This is very fucked up, he thought.

In the next room, hidden behind a one-way wall wired with tiny cameras, two ASI agents were watching Starr intently. They were armed with Chromebooks and top-secret Apple earbuds, their eyes darting between the screen and Starr's reactions.

They were both doctors in military psychiatry, and experts in plain old spy craft. But they were not the creators of this meta-flood of images. The lightning quick barrage of nonsense was coming from ASI's top-secret AI program called Automated Neural Generative Enhanced Learning. It represented something far beyond the cutting edge of the world's best-known available artificial intelligence programs.

The AI program was also compiling a montage of Starr's micro-expressions, creating an on-the-spot visual map of his subconscious. The resulting compilation was projected onto a large screen in front of the agents, showing a clear progression of Starr's thoughts and emotions.

"This is the pattern that's consistent," one agent said, pointing to the screen. "He's definitely reacting to that one specific image. That weird satellite AI made up."

The other agent nodded, her eyes narrowing as she studied the data.

"I wonder why . . ." she said.

Ten minutes later, Starr was in the lobby of the massive A-Frame, standing at the reception desk and looking around for someone to help him. He needed a secure line out immediately—and a little lunch wouldn't hurt.

But nobody was there.

He stood at the empty desk for another two minutes, but still no one appeared. In fact, there was no one at all inside the giant lobby, guests or staff.

Where the hell was everybody?

He'd returned to his room right after his last session, desperate to get his secure phone to work, but by now, it was simply dead. His mind was racing, replaying the events of the past thirty minutes, trying but failing to make sense of it all.

Now he was being victimized by poor customer service? Or actually, none at all.

This was not good for him psychically or physically, so he decided there was only one thing left for him to do.

But he'd have to be careful.

Chapter Seven

The late afternoon sun cast a golden glow over the ASI compound, bathing the lush gardens in a warm light. Starr stepped out of the facility, the fresh air a welcome contrast to the sterile environment he had been confined to.

He started off briskly, heading for the far end of the gardens. He felt the weight of the Tomato Can in his pocket. It was reassuring. Desperate to hear her voice and find some semblance of normalcy, he was looking to find a secluded spot to call Angel.

Around one corner, there was an isolated bench, out of view of the rest of the garden. But just as he was about to activate the old sat-phone, a cheerful voice called out to him.

"Lieutenant Starr!"

It was Kelly Kosmo-Bolo, his guide, waving to him and approaching with a radiant smile.

He immediately ditched the Tomato Can. She was in front of him a few seconds later.

"I'm glad I found you," she said. "You're already late for your next session."

His heart dropped hearing that. He wasn't too sure how much more of this he could take.

"Sorry," he said. "I just had to sneak out of my room and get some air . . ."

"I understand that," she said, her smile widening. "It's a beautiful afternoon and some fresh air would be a nice change of pace for you."

She pulled out her cell, typed a message at lightning speed, and hit send. The reply came back instantaneously. "They've delayed your next session by fifteen minutes."

"I didn't even know I had another test today," he told her. "I thought I was done until five tomorrow morning."

She just laughed. "That's how it is around here. One test always leads to another and another. It's like being on a hamster wheel. Very frustrating, I'm sure."

They started walking, Kelly leading him through a winding path that meandered through the heart of the ASI compound. The gardens were meticulously maintained, with a variety of exotic plants and flowers in full bloom. The scent of jasmine and roses filled the air, creating a serene atmosphere.

Starr figured, if he was ever going to have a bitch session with her, now was the time.

"Just for the record," he began, "the secure phone in my room does not work. I've tried it many times, it's dead."

Out came her cell again, sending another lightning text.

"Anything else?" she asked him.

He didn't expect her question, so he had to think a moment.

"Well, a snack or something would be nice . . ."

More furious texting.

"And I really didn't think I'd be going through this battery of tests. I was under the impression that this was some sort of relaxation retreat."

One last text, two seconds go by, and she gets a reply. "It says: we are working to solve all of these issues. Your next test is in ten minutes."

She started leading him back towards the big A-Frame.

"This path is known as the 'noodle way,'" she said, gesturing to the winding trail ahead. "It's designed to mimic the intricate patterns of noodles, symbolizing the twists and turns of life. But also, the golf cart paths that run all over Catalina. You must have seen them flying in."

Starr nodded. "I sure did. And that's quite poetic. I can see how it fits."

They continued along the winding path, eventually arriving at a picturesque pond. In the center, a bright yellow submarine bobbed gently on the water's surface.

"That's our Yellow Submarine," Kelly explained. "It's a popular attraction here. Guests can take it out on the pond and explore the underwater world."

Starr raised an eyebrow. "Underwater world? In a pond?"

Kelly laughed. "It's not just any pond. There's a whole ecosystem down there, carefully curated to mimic a miniature ocean. It's quite fascinating."

It was fascinating. But all Starr could think of was: who paid for all this?

"And over there," she said, pointing to a sleek, futuristic vehicle parked near a clearing, "is our air taxi. It's the primary mode of transportation around the island."

Starr nodded, impressed. "I know. I've witnessed it first-hand. It was quite a ride."

Kelly smiled again, repositioning her enormous eyeglasses a little. "It's efficient and eco-friendly," she said. "And, of course, offers stunning views of Catalina."

He asked her: "Do you know they're shooting a UFO movie out there?"

The abrupt change in topic caught her off guard, a first.

"A UFO movie?" she asked.

He explained what he saw while flying to the ASI retreat. Crashed saucer, movie lights, people dressed in military garb, lots of gasoline-powered vehicles.

She consulted her cellphone then began nodding enthusiastically. Suddenly, she was very excited.

"Yes! They're using the island's unique landscape to create some incredible scenes," she told him. "I hear it's quite a production."

The walk ended as soon as they passed beneath a gazebo, nestled among towering trees and vibrant flowers to face the giant A-Frame once again.

Kelly turned to Starr, her expression softening. "I hope you enjoyed our walk and talk as much as I did, Lieutenant Starr. Sometimes, it's nice to take a step back and appreciate the beauty around us."

Starr nodded. "It was great . . ."

"So, can I bring you to your next session?" she asked him.

"Can you give me five more minutes?" he asked her. "I can meet you in the lobby."

Her smile was warm and genuine. "Of course. See you in a few."

Once he was sure she was out of sight, he found another secluded bench under a canopy of trees. He glanced around to ensure he was alone before pulling the Tomato Can from his pocket.

His heart pounded as he dialed Angel's number, praying for a clear connection.

The phone rang once, twice – ten times.

But there was no answer, no voicemail. She was supposed to stay home all weekend.

Where could she be?

Chapter Eight

Nine minutes later, Starr was back in the sub-basement of the A-Frame, and back inside Viewing Cube 6.

Once again, the interior was box-shaped, stark and utilitarian. A large TV screen dominated one wall. He sat down to find a hand-held remote resting on one arm of the recliner-like seat. But it had only a single control on it: a large red button. Push it for on, un-push it for stop.

Suddenly the lights went down low; Starr's eyes took a moment to adjust.

"Just push the on button when you're ready," a voice from nowhere explained.

He did as asked.

The monitor flickered to life, revealing a grainy video feed of . . . Angel's bedroom. Starr couldn't believe it. An invasive camera was capturing the room in sharp, colorful detail.

Then Angel entered from the left, obviously unaware she was being watched. Suddenly, a man enters from the right. Incredibly, Angel smiles at him. He leans in to kiss her. Starr's heart began pounding out of his chest. The man and Angel undressed each other, their movements slow and sensual. Starr's vision blurred with helplessness at this point. He hit the button, and the video stopped.

A sudden knock on the door jolted him back to reality. It creaked open, and a new researcher stepped inside. She too was a knock-out, but he hardly noticed. He was about to lay into her with rarely displayed fury. The violation of privacy and intimacy was miles off the charts. And for what?

But she beat him to the punch.

"That concludes this session of regressive therapy," she said. "This was just an exercise to test your mental reflexes ahead of your panel of tests tomorrow."

He had to think a moment. Then he repeated weakly: "Just an exercise?"

"Yes, that's right," she replied almost quizzically. "It's all made up. Nothing here is real. You were watching something generated by AI for your specific needs. I don't know what was on it—no one does but you. I was just measuring your reactions."

Chapter Nine

Starr staggered back to his room, unescorted.

He collapsed on the bed, a steady buzz now ping-ponging inside his skull. It was so bad, he would have suspected they were drugging his food or drink, but he'd had none of either. His mind was reeling that they would come up with something like that to show him. Fake or not, it broke every ethical standard in the book.

He had to call Angel immediately. But his outside secure line was still dead. Screw this, he said out loud. He reached deep into his travel bag and retrieved his Tomato Can.

His hands shook as he activated the phone. He had just witnessed a video that shattered his reality—a fake voyeuristic recording showing Angel with another guy. He *had* to talk to her.

The phone rang once, twice, three times. No answer. His anxiety escalated with each ring when suddenly it went to voicemail.

"Angel, it's Chris," he said, his voice shaky. "I need to talk to you. Please call me back as soon as you get this. I need to know you're okay."

He ended the call and threw the phone onto the bed, running his hands through his hair in frustration.

Maybe it was time for a change of careers.

Angel was lying in bed, her Tomato Can under some clothes on the bureau, out of sight. Suddenly, she stirred, her eyes fluttering open, and saw its missed call notification blinking.

Jumping out of bed, she gathered the sat-phone and hurried into the other room. Seeing two missed calls from Starr, her heart sank.

She tried calling him back but couldn't get a good signal. After more than a dozen attempts, she gave up. She never missed a call from him, and she knew he wouldn't have called unless he needed her.

She carefully hid the Tomato Can again and slowly walked back into the bedroom, feeling a deep gloom.

In the dark, another woman's voice asked her softly, "What's wrong?"

No sooner had Starr put the sat-phone back in his travel bag when he heard a gentle beeping. It was the Tomato Can—someone was calling him.

Angel . . . please . . .

He answered it—but it was not Angel.

It was a disembodied voice, sounding like it was being broadcast from back in the 1930s, crackly and full of static. It was a strange message. "The owners of the last haunted house you were in have a proposition for you. They'll help you out of your present situation, if you help them out with an issue of theirs."

All he really heard was "they'll help you out of your present situation" and at the moment he couldn't have wanted anything more. And he was fairly certain the call wasn't coming from within the ASI compound. Why would those people be calling him on his Tomato Can? Weird stuff happened all the time in his world of spies and bad guys. And sometimes getting a new, more important assignment was a way to get out of a really shitty one. Though it was worrisome that the mystery voice had called the Tomato Can.

Still, all he could think of was to say: "I'm listening . . ."

The voice gave him a set of coordinates. "You will meet an asymmetrical aircraft at that location at 0100 hours. It's about a mile from your present location. Can you make it?"

He felt a sudden surge of energy go through him.

"Repeat those coordinates," he said. "And I'll be there."

Chapter Ten

It was exactly midnight when Starr made his move. Taking only the Tomato Can and his sidearm, he slipped out into the corridor and headed for the emergency stairway.

He supposed he'd been subconsciously preparing for this moment since he'd arrived at ASI, his mind's eye always looking for the quickest way out.

As luck would have it, a commotion of sorts was happening outside in the parking lot. He could hear and feel people running in the direction of all the fuss. This was timely as it gave him another distraction to aid in his escape.

Playing it cool, he walked to the nearest stairwell and then slipped inside. He immediately started going down, his pre-cog abilities guiding him around or under every security cam he came to.

Undetected to the ground floor, he went down one more after that to the sub-basement. In a situation like this, when you wanted to get out of somewhere, his training said find out where they take out the trash and exit that way. It is usually unguarded. At the far end of the corridor where he'd had the two mind-blowing sessions, he recalled seeing a door marked: Refuse Only.

That was his objective.

Sliding out of the stairwell, he found the hallway empty. The harsh fluorescent lights overhead flickering ominously as he approached the Refuse door, hugging the walls here, running in a crouch there, taking advantage of all the blind spots out of view of the security cams. He didn't think many people would actually want to escape from this place, especially through the basement, so the security cameras here were few and far between and they mostly covered intersections.

Still, it sent chills down his spine when he passed by the Viewing Cube 6. He didn't know which session there had been more upsetting, his STPA-2 catching the mysterious satellite image, or what was real but not real about the scene in Angel's bedroom. He had to avert his eyes when he went by the garishly red door. The impact had been that deep.

He reached the door marked Refuse, and very gently felt the doorknob. It wasn't locked and he didn't detect any heat along the door frame to indicate there was an alarm.

He took a deep breath and opened it to find . . . Kelly Krono-Bolo, her glasses two inches away from his nose, staring back at him.

Nearly 20 stories up, a caravan of food carts had just come off the elevator and was now stopped in front of Room 1313.

The head of the ASI crafts services was gently rapping on the door and whispering "Lieutenant?" through the cracks. When he got no response, he called someone who gave him the go-ahead to do something. He told the other waiters to look away, then he typed a number into the room's automatic door lock. It swung open with a squeak.

Not waiting to be prompted, the waiters rolled the six food carts into the room. They contained each of the three themed dinners, a Lobster Lunch and an entire tray of breakfast offerings, including a bucket of bacon. The sixth cart held nothing but Avian water and an assortment of beers.

But it was quickly clear that the room was empty. At that point, the service manager called another number and just said: "We have an opening in Room 1313."

Chapter Eleven

That face. That smile. That body, those glasses. They were all hanging on a meat hook in front of him, lifeless eyes fixed forever in an expression of surprise.

It was Kelly, but it wasn't. The truth was even scarier. It was the outer body of a robot, an automaton, something not human.

He tried not to look at it, in the dim light of the corridor, the shadows making the whole thing even more monstrous. He'd had no idea that robot technology had reached a point where they would be indistinguishable from humans. That alone was frightening.

He activated the Tomato Can's flashlight and now saw the entire room. This was a scene that really made his blood run cold. The refuse room was vast, its high ceilings and dim lighting casting eerie shadows over the hideous tableau within. Hanging from the rafters, like macabre decorations, were more human exteriors—skins that had once encased the robotic forms of someone's creations. Others were grotesquely stuffed into refuse bins, still others slumped over trash cans, their empty eye sockets staring into nothingness.

Starr staggered forward, his mind struggling to process the horror before him. His footsteps echoed in the cavernous space, each step bringing him closer to the realization that Kelly Krono-Bolo, his guide and confidante at ASI, had not been human.

He moved deeper into the room, eyes darting from one discarded skin to another. The sheer number of them was overwhelming, a silent army of the artificial and the damned. These things are so disposable? he thought. When done, you just throw them away?

He stumbled upon a refuse bin overflowing with nothing but dismembered faces. The sight of those lifeless parts, once part of something meant to mimic life, stopped him in his tracks.

He could hear the dead, that much everyone knew.

But where do robots go when they die? Could he hear them from the other side, too?

He didn't want to find out.

Finally, his eyes landed on a door at the far end of the room. It was partially concealed by a stack of bins, but it was unmistakably an exit. Starr moved towards it, his legs feeling like lead.

Reaching it, his hands trembled as he fumbled with the handle. It swung open, revealing a narrow staircase leading upwards. Starr felt a glimmer of hope. He started to ascend, two at a time, his footsteps echoing in the confined space.

As he climbed, the weight of what he had seen pressed down on him. The revelation that Kelly was a robot, that the ASI facility might be filled with these artificial beings masquerading as humans, was almost too much to bear. But Starr knew he had to keep moving. He had to get back to Angel, he had to make some sense of all of this.

The staircase seemed endless, but finally, he reached the top. He pushed open another door, and the fresh air washed over him. At last, he was out of the house of horrors.

Now just one more mountain to climb: the compound's outer wall. He ran a zig-zag course to this barrier finding it to be a combination of old chain link fence with hundreds of electrical wires running through it. He saw one lock, though. It was on the gate where the trash was picked up, robotic or otherwise.

With a mixture of stealth and brute force, Starr managed to disable the electronic lock and slip through.

And just like that, he was outside the strange and disturbing place and staring up at the night sky.

The stars had never looked so beautiful.

Chapter Twelve

Catalina was sparsely populated; there were only so many zillionaires in the world. It was also heavily restricted in terms of vehicular access, with golf carts being the primary means of transportation.

For Starr, that meant if he got a head start, it was unlikely anyone would chase him on the ground in anything that could exceed 15 MPH.

He pulled out the Tomato Can and punched in the coordinates given to him. Its crude GPS function indicated he had to go about a mile south, near the Airport in the Sky, the island's only civilian airstrip. Located on a high plateau and typically closed at midnight, Starr appreciated the strategy behind this as a pick-up point. Given its remote location and rugged terrain, it was less likely to be under surveillance or security cameras. It was a good place for a quick getaway.

As he emerged into the open air, the vast expanse of wilderness bordering the ASI facility greeted him. The full moon cast long, pale shadows across the weathered landscape. The wind carried the scent of pine and the distant sound of rushing water. He took a moment to orient himself. The dense forest ahead promised cover but also contained unknown dangers. He decided to stick to the underbrush, moving with the caution of a seasoned predator, every sense on high alert.

Suddenly, a distant rumble reached his ears, distinct and rhythmic. Starr paused, straining to identify the source. The sound grew louder, and soon he felt the ground beneath his feet begin to tremble. Cresting a ridge, he looked down into a wide valley and saw them: a small herd of bison, their dark, hulking forms galloping as one across the open plain. The sight was both awe-inspiring and intimidating. Starr knew he had to pass through the valley, but one wrong move could startle the herd into a stampede that could easily trample anything in its path.

Crouching low, he began to make his way around the edge of the valley, staying downwind and out of sight. The bison had stopped for the moment and were grazing peacefully, their heads buried in the tall grass. The occasional snort or grunt punctuated the otherwise serene scene.

It took ten minutes, but he avoided the herd by going around it. This brought him to another high ridge. He could see the glow of lights on the other side.

He crawled to the top and looked down. In the next valley, they were filming the UFO movie. The set looked just as he'd seen it the day before: a flying saucer-shaped craft embedded sideways in the rocky sand, movie lights, and people in camouflage uniforms surrounding it. The HumVees and other military-style trucks were still there. The only new element was a very large tow truck, positioned right next to the trapped UFO.

He gave the movie set a wide berth and was soon within sight of the Airport in the Sky. It was indeed closed for the night, but he could see most of the remote airstrip nestled atop a plateau. It looked like a terribly lonely place at the moment.

The coordinates were about a quarter mile south of the airport, on a smaller but slightly higher plateau. Here, he believed a helicopter would be waiting to whisk him away from Catalina.

He walked for another ten minutes, found the second smaller plateau, and power-ran to the top. But the flat summit was empty. While it looked like the perfect place to land a chopper, there was no aircraft, no personnel, nothing.

Then he felt something—the air seemed electrified. Things started shimmering. He suddenly felt very warm inside. Looking up, he saw the faint outline of an aircraft maybe 20 feet above him. His heart leaped, adrenaline surging through his veins. He could hear no noise and see no lights, but he knew it was there.

"What the . . ." he started to exclaim.

Suddenly, his Tomato Can started beeping.

It was Angel.

She was in tears, relieved to have finally reached him. But besides saying hello, Starr went silent. He'd waited all this time to talk to her, but at this moment, something else was happening, maybe even bigger than them finally getting in touch.

Because, suddenly hovering above him, was a *real* UFO.

"I'm sorry, honey," he finally said. "But I'll have to call you back."

The aircraft's metallic body shimmered under the moonlight as it hovered silently above the ground. It was completely unlike any human-made craft Starr had ever seen. And nothing like the crashed movie prop the next valley over.

Before he could react, a blinding light enveloped him. Two hooks that looked like tenacles grabbed him under his arms and he felt himself being lifted off the ground, his body seemingly weightless in the beam. He struggled, but his movements were futile against the forces pulling him upward. His mind raced, his thoughts a chaotic whirlpool of astonishment and disbelief.

Then, everything went black.

When Starr regained consciousness, he found himself lying on a cold, metallic floor. He groaned and sat up, his head throbbing. The room was stark and futuristic, filled with advanced technology he couldn't even begin to understand. Smooth metallic surfaces surrounded him, and soft blue lights cast an eerie glow.

As soon as he got to his feet, a door slid open, and three figures entered. They were tall, with elongated limbs and large, almond-shaped eyes that glowed softly. Starr's heart almost stopped. He was face-to-face with aliens.

"Welcome, Lieutenant Starr," one of the beings said in a surprisingly human voice. Its mouth didn't move, but the words resonated in his mind.

Starr's military training kicked in, his instincts screaming at him to stay calm and assess the situation. "Where am I? What do you want with me?"

"We are here to help you," the being replied. "And you are safe."

Starr began to question his sanity. He took a step back, scanning the room for any possible escape routes. The beings moved closer, their movements fluid and unthreatening.

But suddenly, the room began to spin and the figures wavered like images on a screen. Starr blinked, and the scene before him changed completely. The aliens disappeared, their bodies turning to small clouds of gold dust. The room's metallic surfaces remained, but the eerie glow and futuristic elements were gone.

It hit him like a sledgehammer. This wasn't a UFO. It was a hologram, a sophisticated illusion.

"Impressive, isn't it?" a voice said from behind him.

Starr turned to see the most unlikely character of all. It was Agent Conrad, the high-level DARPA operative who nearly ended Starr's career.

"You?" Starr growled. "What the hell is going on?"

Conrad smiled, an odd look for him. He stood about 6 feet tall with a lean but muscular build, ramrod straight posture, oft-broken nose with weathered skin and a few scars on his face. He looked like the villain in every bad horror movie ever made.

"Welcome aboard the DARPA surveillance and cloaking balloon," he said, the smile vanishing quickly. "AKA the Advanced Nano-technology Geospatial Environmental Locator. We needed to get you off Catalina without raising a fuss. The UFO disguise? Just a little extra insurance."

"So, this entire thing was a setup?" Starr asked him, anger creeping into his voice.

"Not at all," Conrad replied. "Let's just say the ASI facility had plans for you that didn't align with our interests and were certainly not as important. We needed you, and this was the only way to extract you without triggering their alarms."

Almost a year before, Starr had volunteered to be locked inside a purportedly haunted house, a place where they filmed a TV reality show, which had been the site of some mysterious disappearances. Even he admitted some very unusual things took place while he was trapped inside but it all turned out to be an elaborate hoax, created by the top-secret government agency known as the Defense Advanced Research Projects Agency, or more simply, DARPA.

They were known as the Pentagon's mad scientists and for good reason: they had created everything from stealth technology to the Internet to GPS to wearable exoskeletons that could turn the most typical soldier into The Hulk. They'd also created pigeon-guided nuclear weapons, a mechanical elephant and Agent Orange. The Haunted House Hoax was part of an experiment to see if the American public could be brainwashed simply by watching something on TV and when Starr found out about it, Conrad was able to manipulate events to make it seem like Starr himself was the villain.

Starr escaped with his career, but just barely. For this and other reasons, he detested Conrad.

He forced himself to stay calm, though. "And what do you need me for?"

Conrad's expression turned serious. His whole body slumped. His eyes even began to get watery.

"It's a job we feel only you can do," he said. "And we are prepared to brief you immediately."

The invisible DARPA spy balloon was a triumph in MCT, or metamaterial cloaking technology.

It was about half the size of the Goodyear blimp and was shaped more like an overly inflated triangle than a giant flying cucumber. Its topside was layered with thousands of light sensors, its bottom with thousands of illuminative filaments. The sensors on the top essentially gathered light from the night sky stars, clouds or anything in between—and then projected it onto the blimp's underside. This was done so precisely, a ground-based observer wouldn't be able to tell that the blimp was passing right over their heads.

The amazing thing was, other than the slightest, occasional sway, there were no indications that they were flying in a balloon just a few hundred feet above the ground. The craft was incredibly stable.

The control room was on the leading tip of the triangle, one compartment forward from where Starr found himself when he first came aboard. It was small, but not cramped and like what Starr had seen aboard LCACs—huge hovercrafts the Marines used for getting equipment ashore. Two pilots were handling the blimp's helicopter-like controls; several other crewmembers were watching over an array of spy cameras and various surveillance instruments. Despite the reasons for his being here, Starr was blown away by the amazing technology.

Agent Conrad was clearly in command. A smaller compartment off the control room was his office. Desk, chair, bunk, TV. Spartan didn't even come close.

Starr was sitting inside this room now, facing the TV monitor. Conrad sat behind his small desk, a remote control in hand.

"Watch and then discuss," he said.

The screen came alive with extraordinarily clear nightscope video of a helicopter attack on a building in the middle of a ravaged war zone. In the lower right-hand corner, it simply said: Demask, Ukraine. The footage was so crisp it looked like an action movie.

The helicopters were Mi-24 Hind gunships. Starr followed along as the first copter fought through a hail of gunfire only to get torn apart on landing by opposing gunmen. With the wreck in flames and many KIAs scattered around it, a second Hind came in, soldiers pouring out of it, quickly eliminating any threats on the roof.

The scene then shifted to footage coming from the Go-Pro camera attached to one of the attacking soldiers' helmets. It followed them down a stairwell where more bloody fighting took place. Suddenly the scene shifted again to, incredibly, an X-rated pay-for-view porn site, which showed a young girl in the process of taking her top off when masked soldiers break into her room and carry her away.

Returning to the helmet-cam, the attacking soldiers climbed back to the roof, and back in the waiting helicopter, the sky above and around it filled with tracer rounds streaking by in every conceivable direction. The copter lifted off but was hit almost immediately by a large anti-aircraft round of some kind.

The pilots did their best to keep the gunship airborne, but it was a lost cause. It crashed on top of some trenches on the edge of the small town and burst into flames. While that would have seemed to be the end of it, incredibly two people can be seen crawling out of the flaming wreckage. It was a soldier and the young girl taken from the building.

They dropped down into the nearest trench and started running. A few seconds later, they were lost in the darkness and the smoke.

Quickly putting two and two together, Starr said to Conrad: "Don't tell me you want me to go to Ukraine?"

But the DARPA officer didn't reply. Instead, he started a new video rolling on the TV monitor.

It was of a live pay-to-view X-rated porn site, the same one shown in the building attack video where the soldiers snatch the young girl. But while that footage concentrated on that one girl in that one room, what he was seeing now was a grid showing twenty different locations with twenty different girls, all young, sultry and all looking miserable.

The name of this site was Chazter-Bate and the idea was you paid a fee, and the girl of your choice will bring you into a "private room" for ten minutes and let nature take its course. But Starr realized he was looking at just one grid of twenty girls. There were more than *300* grids to choose from. That meant at that very moment, more than 6,000 girls were involved in this enterprise at 6,000 different locations. The scope of it was amazing.

But then Conrad went to an exclusive section of the website called the Diamond Room. It cost five hundred tokens to get in (at one dollar each) but somehow Conrad had the password.

What Starr saw was mostly more of the same, a grid full of sultry females, except the girls here were barely teenagers, if at all. Each grid square featured a prominent smiley face in the upper left-hand corner. Some were pulsating, some were not. There was an empty room on the first page grid and Starr recognized it as the same place the young girl had been snatched from.

He felt like he'd already broken a number of laws just looking at all this. Porn was porn, but this was something else. Finally, Conrad chose to speak.

"It's very important that we recover the girl seen taken in that video," he told Starr. "Those were Spetsnaz troops assaulting that building, and as you saw for yourself, it looks like that girl survived that crash. Where she is now, we don't know. We have a number of assets looking for her and hopefully it will be just a matter of time before we pick up her trail, but as of this moment, that hasn't happened."

More basic math and Starr asked him, "So, you want me to go in and find this girl?"

Conrad nodded. "Yes, we do . . ." he said.

Starr just shrugged and asked him: "Why?"

Conrad hesitated for a moment.

Then he took a long breath and said: "Because she's my daughter . . ."

Chapter Thirteen

Angel was suddenly awake.

She'd laid down earlier, cradling her Tomato Can, wishing with all she had that Starr would call her back.

And now, the obsolete sat-phone was beeping.

He started off by saying; "I'm so sorry . . ."

But she hushed him and became teary-eyed again, now with joy, that they were finally back in touch. She'd been so worried about him even before he left for the weekend retreat; not hearing from him for almost a day caused some high anxiety. But now all that was washed away because he was on the phone talking to her.

All she wanted to know was when he was coming home. She was disappointed to learn that it wouldn't be anytime soon.

"You remember that guy Conrad from DARPA?" he asked her.

She did, all too vividly. Not only did he almost wreck Starr's career, but he'd also threatened their relationship as well. "He's a snake," she replied.

"No argument there," Starr agreed. "But he's a snake in trouble at the moment and needs me for a special project. And he managed to get me out of that resort to do it for him. For that alone, I might owe him a favor."

"What kind of special project," she asked.

He almost laughed.

Then he asked her: "Are you sitting down?"

He told her as much as he could. Starting with the utter weirdness of the ASI compound, through to his escape and meeting Conrad again. He told her of the invisible spy balloon, its incredible capabilities and tried to explain what Chazter-Bate was. Her head was spinning by the end of it—as was his.

She had one question. He was being asked to risk his life to rescue the daughter of a guy who nearly killed him in more ways than one, that she understood. But was this really a matter of national security?

Or someone high up in the spy game who had many resources at his disposal to try to get his wayward child back?

Starr actually had the answer as this had been his first question to Conrad as well.

The girl was a runaway. Conrad lived in Hollywood, of all places, and revealed that Nadia, his daughter, had grown up with a bunch of young show-biz brats. He was a single father, and this did not sit well with him, but by his own admission he was away from home more often than not, a well-paid nanny left in charge of young Nadia.

Nadia went out one night and never came back. Instead of calling the police, Conrad hired the best special ops detectives money could buy. He also used every spy and surveillance instrument he could find to look for her—but they all turned up empty. Conrad said he continued an exhaustive search on his own, got lucky and spotted her on Chazter-Bate.

That put the rescue effort in motion, with Conrad knowing that Starr's detective abilities as well as his odd kind of ESP, made him the guy to lead the search.

And the question of National Security?

If Nadia fell into the wrong hands (not that she hadn't already) and her accosters found out who her father was, countless highly classified projects and programs could be compromised.

What would he give up to get his daughter back alive?

Like any father, good or bad, he said he'd give up anything and everything.

By his own admission, *that* was the security risk.

"A young girl is in danger," Angel told him once he was done. "Now, true, there are a lot of young girls in danger around the world. But if we know of one, we can't refuse to help her because so many others are still in danger."

"I couldn't have said it better," Starr replied.

He told her he'd be in touch either by secure phone or, if all else failed, by Tomato Can. They exchanged I-love-you's and then he was gone.

She cradled the obsolete sat-phone for a few moments longer and then finally set it aside.

She'd fallen asleep earlier in the clothes she'd been wearing before all this happened. Now it was finally time to get undressed.

She began to untie the heavy hood and cloak. In another place and time, this ethereal, flowing garment billowed even in the absence of wind and had faint, intricate patterns that seemed to shift and change constantly, much like the surface of a disturbed pool of water.

She finally let it drop to the ground. Underneath she was wearing a plain plaid shirt, blue jeans and an apron. She also stripped them off.

Naked, she walked into the shower and began the hour-long process of washing all the pixie dust out of her hair.

Part Two

Chapter Fourteen

St. Ivan's Monastery
Demask, Ukraine

The monk answered the door after three distinctive knocks.

He opened it to find a soldier wearing an unmarked camouflaged uniform and a large battle helmet and carrying a futuristic rifle with a million gadgets attached.

"It's not the pot, it's the porn . . ." the monk said.

". . . that makes Jack a dull boy," the soldier answered.

Code phrases authenticated; the monk held out his hand. "Sergeant Andy Mercer, SAS . . ."

"Lieutenant Chris Starr," he replied, shaking his hand. "U.S. Naval Intelligence."

The monk hurried him inside and quickly closed the door.

"Welcome to our little piece of nowhere," he said.

Starr was sure he made for a strange sight. He was wearing a full body armored combat suit made from Kevlar and ceramic plates and camouflaged in shades of grey and black for night operations. On his head was an oversized Fritz helmet equipped with built-in Night Vision Goggles or NVGs. In his hands an M-4HBO laser rifle, a still top-secret weapon capable of precision targeting both in close and at substantial distances. Starr was also carrying his Glock 19 in a holster on his hip and a switchblade in his boot.

He'd been dropped off at 0400 hours that morning, right before dawn, by another DARPA surveillance balloon, this one stationed at the NATO base near the city of Orzysz in Poland, close to the border with Ukraine. His insertion was not as dramatic as when he'd been brought aboard the spy balloon over Catalina Island. This one was just a fast rope down to the top of a small hill on the outskirts of Demask, done quick when no one was looking. (The flight over from the U.S. in a specially adapted extra-long-range F-15/EX had been much more exciting, at least in his head. Traveling faster than the speed of sound for several hours without stopping had an almost amphetamine-like effect on him. Translation: he was wide awake.)

But things became difficult right away. The fighting between the Russians and the Ukrainians in this sector was so insane, it took him nearly a half day just to reach the monastery, even though it was only about a mile away from his drop point.

It was that crazy. He'd seen his share of combat zones over the past few years, but nothing like this. The landscape looked like a painting by Bosch on a bad day. Drones, high-velocity weapons, hyperbaric bombs, jet planes, tanks, IEDs, lots of helicopters and lots of brutal hand-to-hand combat—welcome to trench warfare for the 21st century. It had to be the worst way to fight a war if that was even possible. And suddenly it was going on all around him.

He had a card on him, written in Ukrainian and signed by the country's defense minister that ID'd him as *druzny sposterigach nato*—a "friendly NATO observer." He didn't expect any trouble from the Ukrainians—it was the Russians he had to worry about. To be caught by them out here would have staggering implications, mostly for him. So, most of the day he'd spent moving from one abandoned trench to another, avoiding Russian patrols and hiding from their drones. It was only when the sun started to set that he was able to work in the shadows and finally make his way here.

Losing twelve hours at the get-go wasn't the best way to start any mission, but especially not one so time sensitive as this. There was a big clock ticking here. Because of the spy balloon's security procedures, it could only come into the area for short amounts of time and never on a predictable timetable. For him that meant he had to be back at his drop-off point at exactly 0400 hours the next day for his extraction. If he missed it, there was no way of telling when the balloon could come back. And as no one else was supposed to know he was out here, he'd be stuck for a ride home.

But in the meantime, he could not contact anyone. No one at DARPA, no one at the U.S. military. And definitely no one on his Tomato Can. In fact, he'd left it hidden in his personal belongings back in San Diego.

For this one, he was truly on his own.

Next to the CD factory, the monastery was just about the only structure still standing around Demask. Both had somehow survived the non-stop warfare so far.

While it seemed to house five monks who cared for the area wounded as best they could, this holy place was actually a cover for a British special operations unit. From the first floor up, it was an abbey. In the basement was an advanced intelligence gathering post manned by five members of the Special Air Service, England's land version of the SEALs. All they knew was that he was here to rescue an extremely high priority person, namely a young girl named Nadia.

Once inside, Starr took off his helmet and took a deep breath. This place smelled heavily of incense.

"What's our status?" Starr finally asked the faux monk.

"Our friend is still alive," Mercer reported. "But he's just barely hanging on."

"And the girl?"

Mercer sighed. "They came for her last night. We didn't know who she was at that time, or even who they were. But we couldn't compromise what's going on here to do anything besides let her go."

Starr just nodded. That was understandable. And it would have been just *too* easy if she had still been here when he finally arrived.

"Any idea why our Russian friend brought her here in the first place?"

Mercer shrugged. "Total coincidence? As far as we can tell, they both thought this was an actual monastery. They still do . . ."

The SAS man led Starr down a dark and winding corridor, stopping at a thick wooden door that was locked on the outside.

"This is our 'guest room,'" he said dryly.

They both looked in the small, barred window to see a man in a Russian special ops uniform, propped up on a bunk, heavily bandaged and babbling to himself.

"He speaks okay English," Mercer said. "But only when he's drunk."

With that, he let Starr into the room, handed him a bottle of wine he'd been carrying under his cassock and then left, closing the door behind him.

The Russian soldier was in bad shape. He was sitting up but listing heavily to the left. His mid-section was wrapped in bloody bandages, his uniform was dirty and frayed. His eyes locked in the thousand-yard stare; he appeared to be middle-aged. But Starr could tell he was barely in his 20s.

Starr opened the bottle of unlabeled red wine, took a healthy swig, and then passed it to the Russian. The wounded man didn't seem puzzled to see someone who was probably an American special ops soldier standing in front of him. However, he was pleasantly surprised that Starr had brought him a bottle of wine.

"Tell me about Nadia," Starr began, taking a seat in the room's only chair. Outside, he could hear rockets and artillery exploding in the early evening.

The Russian soldier took a gulp of wine.

"You are the second person to ask me such a question in two days," he said in passable English. "That lucky girl. So many people are interested in her."

"How did you come upon her?" Starr asked. He already knew how, but he wanted to hear it from the source.

"I was Spetsnaz," the Russian explained wearily. "They sent us to place where CDs were once made, but now is Chazter-Bait place—or it was. You know 'Chazter-Bait'?"

People go online, pay money to see girls take off their clothes. That was the vanilla definition. Starr repeated it back to him.

But the soldier just took another swig of wine.

"You Americans," he said. "You want everything to be 'Rebecca Goes to Sunnyside Farm.' But real world not like that. These girls, appearing on camera while dirty old men play with themselves, is just beginning of long story. These girls are also bought and sold, auctioned off by same people who run those sites."

Starr was surprised to hear this. "Are you saying they're prostitutes?"

The Russian shook his head. "Prostitutes eventually get paid. These girls get nothing. Whoever buys them keeps them, like property, until they grow bored of them."

"And then?"

The Russian shrugged. "They sell them again," he said nonchalantly. "Or send them to heaven."

Starr had to let this sink in. He wasn't so naïve that he didn't think human trafficking and exploitation of children didn't exist. India? China? Pakistan? Russia . . . It was rampant in those countries, to name a few. But he would never have made the leap from the masturbatory hijinks of the Chazter-Bate crowd to that even deeper, darker world. He wondered if Conrad knew about this and just didn't tell him.

"Are you saying Nadia is involved in that?" he asked the soldier.

"Not yet," was the reply. "But it's just a matter of time. That's how whole thing got started."

Starr took the bottle back from the soldier, took another huge swig, and then returned it.

"Tell me everything," he said, wiping his mouth. "Slowly . . ."

The soldier explained that his Spetsnaz unit was fighting in Donetsk when they were suddenly pulled off the line, re-equipped, and given a new mission. They were to conduct a raid on the Demask CD factory, find Nadia, and bring her out.

"A rescue mission?" Starr asked.

"Oh, yes," he replied. "But not for the Kremlin. For a man named Viktor Robotov. He is the devil on Earth. He's got warehouses full of money, made by stepping over the bodies of little people like us. Do you know of him?"

Starr shook his head no. With a name like that he sounded like a second-rate supervillain.

The Russian soldier told him how this Viktor character was able to not only hire an entire Spetsnaz team to do his bidding, but also a helicopter full of Russian conscripts whose only job was to be sacrificed simply to clear the way for the special ops troops to snatch Conrad's daughter. But the Spetsnaz copter was shot down just seconds after taking off from the factory roof, and everyone on board was killed except him and Nadia. He protected her, leading her across the battlefield to this one place of sanctuary.

"I knew Viktor would come for her," the soldier continued. "And sure enough, Satan himself showed up here last night with his own private helicopter and private little army—and even though we are on front line, somehow no one shoots at him the whole time. That's how powerful he is. He can stop a war, for a little while anyway."

"How's the business of this thing work?" Starr asked, still wondering if any of it was really true. "I can't believe it's allowed to continue . . ."

The soldier had a coughing fit, but then went on.

"Here is way it works," he said. "To outside world Chazter-Bate all looks kosher, other than young girls taking their clothes off for pay. But under the radar Chazter-bate puts *special* young girls on its site on regular basis. Wealthy perverts of world know exactly where to look, and they go shopping. They pick ones they like and make an offer, and if they win, they take delivery on her. And just like selling a Picasso at Sotheby's, sometimes they are intended as their own plaything or sometimes to sell to someone just as twisted but for even more money. It's usually a matter of commerce."

"It sounds brutally simple," Starr replied. "But how does Spetsnaz get involved?"

"Robotov is Russian," the soldier explained. "Chazter-bate is Ukrainian. We are at war with Ukraine. When Viktor saw her for first time, he wanted to buy her very badly, but Chazter-Bate refused. The next night, we were landing on their roof."

"But why her?" he finally asked the soldier. "There were dozens of young girls in that place. It was running day and night."

This got a laugh from the soldier. Starr could tell it hurt him, but the Russian couldn't help it.

"I think he did it for greatest reason of all," he proclaimed.

"For money?" Starr asked. What else could it be?

More laughter now from the Russian, though he was quite clearly in pain.

"No, my friend," he told Starr. "I think he did it for love . . ."

Now it was Starr's turn to laugh. "You're saying this Russian arch criminal fell for a young girl from Los Angeles?"

"That's another problem with you Americans," the Russian replied. "You don't believe in romance . . ."

Starr took a moment. The more he learned about all this, the more surreal it became. Who *was* this Viktor Robotov character? He seemed right out of a paperback novel. But to have an entire Spetsnaz unit at his beck and command? That was above and beyond extraordinary power, even in the byzantine world of Russian politics.

"But how can this Viktor be *that* powerful?" Starr asked him, genuinely puzzled.

The soldier replied: "My friend, whether we know it or not, many parts of this planet are somehow caught up in Viktor's web. More than half the illegal weapons sold around the world run through his hands. Assault rifles to jet fighters. There are even rumors he has some nukes hidden away somewhere, some for sale.

"But he's not just an arms dealer. He has no soul, and he wants yours too. And he'll take it, if he decides you're worth the effort. Sex, war, money—he'll use whatever means necessary. It's like quantum entanglement. Once you step into his world, every move you make, every choice, ripples through the lives of everyone connected to you. And it's the same for them. Imagine ringing a bell here and hearing it sound a billion light-years away—what happens to one affects the other, no matter the distance. Einstein called it 'Spooky Action at a Distance.' We're all entangled in this strange and twisted game, caught in a web where the fate of one influences the fate of all."

He took a long belt from the wine bottle.

Starr was impressed. "Did they teach you that at Spetsnaz school in Averkyevo?" he asked.

The soldier had nearly finished the bottle of wine. He wiped his mouth and thought a moment.

"No," he explained weakly. "Before all this, I was PhD graduate student at Moscow School of Applied Physics. Einstein was my hero."

Starr knocked twice on the door. Mercer opened it and let him out.

The Russian soldier had fallen asleep or passed out; either way he had become non-verbal.

"He was of help?" the monk asked Starr.

"Only to tell me the girl has gone way down a very deep rabbit hole," he replied. "You saw her, if just for a little while. Are the things he told me about her true? That she was being bought and sold on that website?"

The monk didn't reply, but indicated Starr should go with him. He brought him to the basement of the monastery and into a room full of PCs and laptops.

"This is our bomb shelter," the monk explained with a grin. It looked more like a man cave to Starr. Trash barrels filled with empty wine bottles, pictures of scantily clad celebrities adorning the stone walls. He was not sure if the SEALs were allowed to hang racy pictures in their secret dug-outs.

"After your people made contact with us, we looked into this whole situation," Mercer told him. "Just to see if we were compromised in any way."

He turned on one of the computers and it immediately opened to the Chazter-Bate Diamond page.

Starr saw the now-familiar gallery of young women and girls, each in her own sad, little box. Most were staring forlornly into the camera, dressed in cheap provocative clothing and looking like they'd like to be anywhere else but there.

Mercer pointed to several boxes that had the image of a smiley face in the lower left-hand corner next to the flag of their country of origin.

"That's the code that means they are for sale," he explained candidly. "When that image begins blinking, the secret auction has begun. Apparently, this Viktor bloke never missed a day of looking at the merchandise, and when he saw one he liked, he'd usually outbid everyone else and won out quickly.

"But since the war started, the Ukrainians have ignored him, choosing to go with some other rich deviant who was not Russian. And Viktor just laid quiet. He still watched, but he didn't bid.

"But then he saw this Nadia –and well? He called her his *tsukerka*—his piece of candy. To many, that's his way of saying he fell in love with her. The next night he had her snatched from the CD factory."

Starr felt what was left of his mojo flat line. This brought up even more issues, never a good thing.

Having the runaway daughter of a DARPA operator wind up in this position was bad enough. But what if Viktor Robotov finds out who she really is? Or what if he knew already? Suddenly Starr wished he was back on Santa Catalina. "Well, she could be anywhere now," he said gloomily.

"Yes, she could," Mercer replied. "But in this case, we happen to know exactly where that is . . ."

Chapter Fifteen

The night arrived heavy and silent as Starr approached the impressive old mansion.

Nestled in the countryside about two miles inside Russian-held territory, its opulence starkly contrasted with the war-torn landscape so close by. Why do some places get bombed to dust and others hardly get a scratch? Maybe that's what precision weapons are all about. Or maybe not.

Whatever the reason, according to the SAS, tonight this manor was to become a beacon of depravity, hosting a glamorous party where the powerful and the severely bent planned to engage in unspeakable acts with girls below the age of consent.

Starr didn't ask Mercer how they knew Nadia had been brought here, but he assumed they'd sent up a drone as soon as Viktor left the monastery and simply followed him. But *why* would Viktor bring Nadia here? If he already owned her, what was the point?

As Mercer explained: "War or not, the unspeakables like to show off their new possessions. Half of it is a prestige thing—like attending an expensive car show or a thoroughbred horse auction.

"And what's the other half?" Starr had asked.

Mercer had shrugged. "Well, these people are also a little like your Hells Angels back in the States. If one of them finds someone he really likes, they tend to, shall we say, pass her around to their friends."

Hearing that certainly added to the acuteness of the situation. Starr had to find the girl quickly, before any of the debauchery started. And should he forget even for one moment that time was ticking away, he had his trusty cheap watch to remind him. He now had it counting down the time before his extraction balloon arrived at the retrieval site. And at the moment he had less than ten hours to get all this done.

Crouched in the shadows near the estate's high, ivy-covered wall, his breath was visible in the cold night air. That the mansion was *behind* the Russian lines was not unexpected. And due mainly to his NVGs and that a lot of the Russian soldiers were drunk as soon as night fell, Starr had managed to breach all their trenches in no man's land and arrive here undetected.

The problem was the place was surrounded by an army of private guards who looked suspiciously like . . . Spetsnaz. At least two dozen of them, all armed up, muscled-up and mic'd-up, they were like extras from a movie, head bandanas, baseball caps and lots of tats. He could also see two Zala drones circling over the place.

Flying low, they were unarmed recon drones tasked with keeping an eye on everything and everybody.

The estate had an eight-foot brick wall surrounding it, with a long heavily guarded driveway leading to the front then around to the back. But on approaching the place, Starr had spotted a section of the wall that was completely obscured with overgrown vegetation. In fact, it was the only point in the circular barrier that had not been defoliated. His NVGs revealed why. A small gate was hidden behind this foliage. It led into the area where the mansion stored its trash for pick up. No one in the army of security guards was watching over it.

"Wow, does it happen *every* time?" he thought aloud. It really was curious how many times he'd seen this before. No matter the size of the locked-down area or the reason it was so heavily secured, no one ever wanted to guard the garbage chute.

Guests were arriving in bullet-proof limousines and SUVs, turning into the driveway about 100 feet north of him. But some were coming in Russian armored vehicles called BMPs. In fact, these mini-tanks were arriving and departing with such frequency it appeared there were being used as shuttle buses for those guests who were faint of heart. But to his advantage, not only did these vehicles make a lot of noise but they also spouted copious amounts of exhaust. The night was chilly, and this carbon monoxide haze tended to hang close to the ground.

So, Starr waited until another BMP came back, loaded with cretins, and used the noise and the smoke to get to and through this vine-entangled gate unseen and then into the adjoining trash shack beyond. Peeking out the shack's front door, he saw a wooden gate about ten feet away. It was closed but its slats were so far apart he could see an enormous, heated swimming pool beyond, a small cumulus cloud of steam rising above it. At the center of this pool was a sculpture of an old man caressing a young girl.

Guess I'm at the right place, he thought.

He left the trash shack and got right up against the gate, peering through its wooden slats with his NVGs. He soon saw just what he was looking for. A guy about his size and shape, stumbling along next to the pool.

Starr went over the gate in one smooth motion, timing his arrival so he landed behind the drunk. One punch to the base of the spine and the guy collapsed, instantly knocked out by the pain. Starr dragged him back out the gate and into the trash shack, carefully closing the door behind him. Then he took off his battle suit and put on the man's tuxedo, dress shirt, pants and expensive Italian leather shoes. It gave him the creeps, especially the shoes. And while he hated to do it, he had to leave behind his battle helmet and his cool M-4 as well. This left him with his Glock, his silencer, and his switchblade.

He took a moment to get his act together, then slowly slid back out the gate and into the misty pool area. Chlorine was thick in the air. So was the smell of pot. He passed more lecherous old men; none of them paid him any mind. So, he went on to step two. Taking a glass of champagne from a roaming server, he coolly joined the party inside.

The interior of the mansion was a low buzz of activity. There were easily several hundred people moving about, mostly old white guys, but also some representing the Middle East, obvious by their dress. No lights were on anywhere. Instead, there were dozens of lit candles and thousands of small digital bulbs twinkling above it all, like stars against the night sky. Violin music and devious laughter floated everywhere, creating an almost surreal atmosphere of luxury and decadence.

Starr blended into the crowd effortlessly, his sharp eyes scanning the room. Even in these darkened conditions, the affluence here was overwhelming. Marble floors, crystal chandeliers, and gold-trimmed everything. Servers in immaculate uniforms moved like graceful ghosts among the guests. Now the air was thick with the scent of expensive perfumes and colognes. And

Starr's senses were telling him that drug activity was also going on nearby, something beyond pot.

He climbed the grand staircase, the focal point of the mansion's lavish if dim interior. From here he had a better view of the ballroom below. His gaze swept the area, noting security personnel discreetly positioned at many strategic points. But there was no sign of the girl, in fact the only females he saw were middle-aged at best.

So where were the others?

Where was Nadia?

A pair of double doors at the far end of the second-floor hall caught his mind's eye. Two uniformed guards stood by them, their posture and alertness indicating something important lay beyond. Starr closed his eyes, begging the cosmos to help him here. Am I close? he whispered under his breath. A quick tingling sensation running through him told him he was.

He made his way down the hallway, passing through the second-floor crowd, casually but purposefully, angling towards the heavily guarded doors. He needed a diversion, though, something to distract the guards' attention long enough for him to slip past.

He saw his opportunity walking right towards him. It was a man who weighed somewhere north of 400 pounds, carrying a bottle of champagne. Starr slyly took out his Glock, gave the silencer one last twist to make sure it was on tight, then noiselessly fired a round into the guy's left kneecap. The victim let out a yelp and crashed to the floor, the champagne going off like a bomb. The commotion drew immediate attention from the dozens of people around him, the guards included.

Working two seconds ahead of everyone else, Starr had seen it all happen like a quick fast forward, allowing him to slip through the unguarded double doors, the screams of pain coming from the guy he just knee-capped echoing in his ears. He found himself in a dimly lit corridor, even darker than the ballroom. There were no twinkling lights here. This hallway was lined with doors on both sides, like two rows of dressing rooms in a huge clothing store. He guessed each door led to a smaller room used for private meetings or mega-illicit activities. He also guessed this was where all the under-age girls were being kept, for the moment anyway.

He moved swiftly but cautiously down this hallway, listening for any sound that might guide him to Nadia. He heard lots of murmuring coming from the tiny rooms, along with some grim laughter and soft weeping, but nothing to indicate Conrad's daughter was within—until he reached the end of the corridor.

The last door on the left. Why was it always the last door on the left? His body began tingling again. He put his ear to the door. He heard muffled voices on the other side. Two men talking excitedly, with the names Nadia and Viktor being spit out in rapid-fire Russian.

He didn't have much time, so that was going to have to be enough for him.

He took a deep breath and kicked the door open. The men fell silent as he stepped inside, his Glock trained on them. They too were dressed in tuxedos, and they were standing next to a huge four poster bed. Tied to its bedposts, a gag across her mouth, her eyes wide with terror, was Nadia.

"Step away from her," Starr commanded the two men, his voice icy and calm. But they hesitated, almost as if they thought this was some kind of joke. So, Starr put bullets into their kneecaps too, causing both men to crumple in extreme pain.

He went quickly to the girl, using his switchblade to cut off her bonds. He helped her off the bed.

She was smaller, younger, more fragile than he'd imagined from her pictures. She was wearing a pastiche of a young girl's school clothes, short here, low-cut there, and tight all around, sexy in the world of Chazter-Bate.

She started to cry, probably thinking the worst.

"It's okay," he whispered to her. "I'm an American and I'm here to get you out . . ."

She was confused, frightened, but now tears of hope were welling up in her eyes. Starr glanced around the room, noting the exits, and calculating their best route of escape. He knew it was only a matter of time before the guards realized something was wrong in here.

"Stay close to me," he told her. "Whatever happens, just stay close . . ."

He chose the door at the furthest end of the room. It led to a servants' corridor located in the back halls of the mansion, a place that the guests would not normally see. They followed it quickly and quietly, Starr holding her hand tight. Finally, they reached a small, dimly lit breakfast kitchen, where a lone server was cleaning up.

The young man looked up in surprise, but Starr silenced him by showing him his pistol.

"*Vi ukrainets?*" he asked him. "Are you Ukrainian?"

"*Tak, moye misto bulo zachoplenie minulogo roku,*" he replied. "Yes, my town was overrun last year."

Starr showed him the fake NATO card.

"We need to get out of here," he told him quietly. "Which way to your trash shack?"

The server hesitated for a moment, but then spoke to them in passable English. "This service entrance leads to the back gardens and then the pool area. The trash station is through the gate at the far end of the pool."

Starr nodded his thanks, glad to be pointed back in the right direction. He led the girl through the kitchen and towards the service entrance.

But while his mind was focused on getting to safety, he couldn't help but think about all the innocents he was leaving behind. This Viktor Robotov seemed genuinely evil, and so were his friends. Starr couldn't just leave all those young victims behind without giving them at least a fighting chance to get out. So just as he and the girl reached the service door, he pulled the mansion's fire alarm. Then as they stepped outside into the empty gardens, he fired five shots from his Glock into a nearby electrical transformer, killing all power inside the place.

Then, they started moving through the cool night air. At the moment, he looked like just another deviant in a tux with a girl dressed up for school. While the chaos began to flare up inside the mansion, they calmly walked through the garden, along the pool, out the gate and back to the trash shack. Just as they got inside, he heard the sound of vehicles approaching in the night. Fire equipment and more BMPs. Reinforcements, no doubt alerted by the commotion inside the mansion. Time to move fast.

Climbing back into his battle suit and retrieving his rifle and oversized helmet, he led the girl out of the trash gate, making sure the coast was clear before they even took a breath. Then behind him, he heard gunshots and people yelling in Russian. He could also see girls and the mansion's help streaming out of the place, shielded by the blaring false alarm. But even in the darkness and bedlam Starr had caused, the guards had discovered Nadia was missing and were now in hot pursuit.

They sprinted towards the nearby woods, the shouts growing louder behind them. Then bullets began whizzing past, but Starr didn't stop, continually urging the girl to stay ahead of him.

They reached the thicket and plunged into the darkness, the dense foliage providing fair cover. Starr maneuvered her through flora, his military training guiding them over the unfamiliar terrain. But he could hear the guards crashing through the underbrush behind them as well.

They ran for what felt like an eternity when the sounds of pursuit gradually faded. Finally, they reached a large hollow covered over by a burned-out willow tree. Starr allowed them to rest under it for a moment. The girl collapsed to the ground, her breathing coming in ragged gasps.

"Are you okay?" Starr asked, kneeling beside her.

She nodded, her eyes still wide with a mixture of fear and gratitude.

"Who are you?" she finally asked him, almost with a nervous laugh.

He thought a moment and then just said: "I'm an associate of your father's."

Now her face displayed a look of sudden shock. "*He* sent you to look for *me*?" she asked, almost in a gasp. "Really?"

He just looked down at her and couldn't help but smile. "Yes, he did . . . really."

It seemed like she was having trouble believing this. But finally, she whispered: "Well, thank you, whoever you are. I never thought I was going to get out of there . . ."

"You're safe now," Starr assured her. "But we need to keep moving."

They climbed out of the hollow and continued jogging through the woods, moving cautiously but steadily. But overhead they could hear the high whine of the Zala recon drones, flying back in forth in a classic search pattern, looking for them. Starr thought for a moment whether he should shoot them down with his M4. The high-tech rifle was quite capable of doing just that, but the resulting crashes would just pinpoint their location to the people looking in on the other end. It would be safer just to avoid them long enough for them to run low on fuel and be forced to return from whence they came.

They finally reached a small road Starr recognized from his earlier recon. Following it, they kept in the shadows until they reached the outskirts of a tiny village, most of it decimated.

There was one small intact brick building, though, another structure that miraculously survived the chaos of war. Its lights were still on despite the late hour. Starr led the girl to a hiding spot near the front door as he covertly peeked in a side window. He saw the back of an old woman, dressed all in black including a veil. This village had been part of Ukraine not two years before. He got out his fake NATO card and knocked quietly on the door. After a moment, it opened, and the elderly woman peeked out.

"Please," Starr said, holding up his card and a hundred-dollar bill and indicating the girl nearby. "We need help."

The woman's eyes widened as she read the card, studied their unusual clothing, and then the crisp $100 bill. She opened the door wider, and only then did Starr realize she was wearing a veil and a long tunic with a set of gigantic rosary beads around her neck.

She was a nun.

Jackpot, he thought.

"Please . . . sister," Starr revamped his request. "I'm trying to save this girl's life."

She ushered them inside. "Come, quickly," she said in English but with a heavy accent.

Silently telling them to be quiet, the nun led them to a small bedroom on the second floor of the building. They neither saw nor heard anyone else.

Once inside, she asked them what was happening, her voice filled with concern.

Starr quickly explained that he was a private investigator and had been hired to bring the girl back home, but they had to lay low somewhere until the Russian drones stopped looking for them. The nun listened, her expression growing more serious with each word.

"You can stay here," she said finally, taking the hundred-dollar bill. "And this will go to the orphans."

"Thank you, sister," Starr said, his voice filled with gratitude. "We just need a couple hours and then we'll be on our way."

She looked at the girl, who was sitting on the edge of the bed, looking exhausted but relieved.

"You should get cleaned up," she told her gently, fingering the naughty schoolgirl outfit. "And get into some other clothes."

She turned back to Starr and said: "Let me take her to the washroom and give her something else to wear and—give her a little privacy. That's probably been lacking for her lately."

"I'll have to stand outside the door," he told her.

She nodded vigorously. "That's mandatory," she replied.

The nun and the girl disappeared behind an oak door right across from the room she'd given them.

Starr took up his position outside this door. Holding his M-4 at his side, he took a moment for himself. Just as it had been wise to give up his borrowed tuxedo for his trusty battle suit, it was a very good idea to get Nadia into something less provocative and noticeable. She'd probably welcome a bath at this point too.

He consulted his backward running watch. It was about 8:00 PM local time. That gave him eight hours to cross back over the Russian lines and make the retrieval spot on time. It was only a mile or so; a long trek in the daytime, but much easier at night. He was hopeful they could still make it in the dark.

A few minutes went by. Starr was waiting to hear the sound of running water or something, but it was all quiet on the other side of the door. He finally took a chance and peeked in.

There was no tub, no wash basin in sight. In fact, the room was empty, its only window left wide open, its dilapidated curtains blowing in the breeze.

"Son of a bitch . . ." he murmured.

The girl and the nun were gone.

Chapter Sixteen

One hour later

Starr stood outside the high stone walls of the Convent of the Bleeding Hearts, the moon casting an eerie glow around the archaic structure. Hidden in thick woods just a mile east of the village, the convent was a relic from another era. And unlike the deviant mansion, as drabby as one could imagine. It was the perfect place to hide something—or someone.

Nadia was now a captive again, this time by a group of nuns apparently in the service of that familiar name: Viktor Robotov. Starr was beating himself up for falling for an old trick. He should never have let Nadia out of his sight—and at this point, it was unforgivable.

He'd mistakenly thought the house they'd sought refuge in was a convent. It turned out to be a brothel. That was clear soon after he realized he'd been duped. Running down the hallway, he kicked in three doors, his Glock out and ready. But in each case, he played the part of *coitus interruptus*. It was a big surprise for him with the first kick-in, to see sexual activity in what he thought was a house of the holy. The second busted door just brought more puzzlement. By the third time, he realized this was definitely not a home for nuns.

But there was a connection. He caught the third John by the scruff of his neck as he was trying to flee. The customer was a low-level Russian officer, getting laid. Or trying to.

The terrified man told him in broken English that the business of the whorehouse was run by the Sisters of the Bleeding Hearts, but they didn't live here. They lived about a mile down the road back to Demask. The man also helpfully indicated that these nuns were not the pious women they pretended to be. Instead, they were ruthless operators of brothels all over this part of Europe, just another part of Viktor's worldwide but secret sex empire.

"You know who Viktor is, right?" the Russian asked him.

Instead of replying, Starr asked him how he got to the village. The man revealed he had a car parked outside. Starr demanded the keys; the man complied, saving himself from getting a 9-mm round in his left patella.

The car was parked out back of the brothel. It was a Russian Lada Granta, only a year old and already falling apart. It was also full of bullet holes, a testament to its former owner and his dangerous unstoppable drive through a war zone to get a little something-something.

Starr had gotten the crappy Russian car up to 80 M.P.H. and absolutely tore up the dirt road driving here, all the while looking for any Russian drones overhead. He was able to glance at his cheap wristwatch, ticking down to when he had to rendezvous with the spy balloon. Just seven and a half hours to go.

He ditched the car on arriving at the convent, and took up a position here, just outside its imposing wall. There was no army of armed guards here, though. He couldn't even see any security cameras though he was sure they were out there somewhere.

Taking a deep breath, he went over the wall, his movements swift and silent. He landed softly on the other side, crouching to avoid detection. The courtyard was dimly lit by a few torches, their flickering light casting long shadows. He moved quickly, sticking to the darkness, his senses on high alert.

Reaching the main building, he found a side door partially hidden by ivy. He carefully picked the lock and slipped inside, entering a long, dimly lit hallway, something he'd been doing a lot of lately. The air was thick with the smell of incense, but underneath it, he detected a faint, metallic scent—blood.

His heart pounded as he made his way through the silent corridors, listening for any signs of life, praying for his extra sensory abilities to lead him in the right direction. He reached a heavy wooden door and pressed his ear against it. Muffled voices and footsteps echoed from the other side. Slowly, he pushed the door open, revealing a large dining hall filled with nuns. They were not praying or having a meal but rather engaging in what looked like a brutal martial arts combat training session. Clad in traditional habits, they weren't just sparring with each other. They were hitting each other with enthusiastic violence, their movements precise and intense.

Starr closed the door. He needed to find Nadia without alerting these women. He reached the far end of the hall and slipped through an old fire escape door, finding himself in a narrow stairway leading down. He descended quickly, his footsteps light on the old wooden steps. The stairs led to a dimly lit basement, the air colder and damper than above. The sound of water dripping echoed in the darkness.

Starr stopped and let his mental acuity take over. At the end of the corridor, he spotted a heavy, iron door. He moved towards it with haste, picked the lock and opened it slowly, revealing a small, dark jail cell. Inside, huddled in a corner, was Nadia, now dressed in an extra-small version of a nun's habit, veil and all.

Her eyes widened with relief as she ran to him.

"Oh my God!" she gasped, falling into his arms and trembling. "These women are monsters!"

"You're okay now," Starr whispered back. He checked her for injuries—she had a few bruises and cuts, but nothing life-threatening. "Can you walk?"

She nodded, her eyes determined. "Yes, I can."

"Okay," he said. "Let's try this again."

They moved back towards the stairway, but as they reached the top, they were confronted by two nuns, their expressions cold and menacing.

"Going somewhere?" one of them sneered in Russian, as each pulled out a wicked-looking carving knife.

Starr pushed Nadia behind him, snapping the safety off his Glock at the same time.

Could he really shoot two nuns?

"Stay back," he ordered them. But the nuns ignored him, lunging simultaneously, their movements eerily synchronized. Starr ducked under the first strike and blocked the second with his forearm, then countered with a quick jab to one nun's throat. She staggered back, choking, but the other nun was already swinging her blade again.

Starr sidestepped that attack and landed a powerful kick to her midsection, sending her crashing into the wall. He swiftly disarmed the first nun and knocked her out with a well-placed punch to the throat.

The second nun tried to rise, but Starr subdued her with a chokehold until she went limp.

He was tempted to kneecap both of them, but he didn't want to waste ammunition.

"Come on," he said to Nadia. "Just stay close."

They ran through the basement corridors, but the commotion had alerted more nuns. As Starr and Nadia reached the main hall, they were confronted by four more nuns, each one bigger, more imposing and meaner looking than the last.

"Again, get behind me," Starr told Nadia, his voice calm but firm.

The nuns advanced, their faces twisted with spite. Starr braced himself, knowing this fight would not be easy. The first nun attacked with surprising speed, her fists aiming for his head. Starr blocked and countered, landing a punch that sent her reeling. The second nun swung a heavy candlestick at him, but he ducked and delivered a powerful uppercut that knocked her to the ground.

The remaining two nuns charged together, using their size and strength to try to overpower him. Starr fought back with everything he had, his training and instincts kicking in. He landed a series of rapid punches and kicks, but the nuns were relentless. One of them grabbed him from behind, trying to choke him, while the other aimed a punch at his ribs.

Starr twisted out of the chokehold and elbowed one nun in the face, breaking her nose. She screamed in pain and fell back, but the other nun tackled him to the ground. They grappled fiercely, rolling across the floor. Then suddenly she was gone, whacked by something with great velocity on the side of her head and falling off to the side with a thud. Starr looked up to see Nadia holding an enormous candlestick.

"God, I *so* don't like nuns anymore," she said.

They moved through the convent, Starr's mind racing while trying to find the quickest route of escape. They reached a courtyard and made their way to the outer wall, but then a voice stopped them in their tracks.

"Leaving so soon?"

Starr turned to see the nun who had hoodwinked him last time. A towering figure with cold, calculating eyes, she was flanked by two more huge nuns, in full habits, each armed with even larger kitchen knives and ready for a fight.

"We don't want any trouble," Starr said, keeping himself protectively in front of Nadia. He pulled out his trusty switchblade, but if he couldn't shoot a nun, could he really *stab* one?

"Trouble has already found you," the head nun replied, running her finger along the sharp edge of her weapon. "You cannot leave here alive, I'm afraid. Those are our orders."

Starr knew there was no reasoning with her. He prepared for the final confrontation, his muscles tensing. The head nun and her companions advanced, their expressions devoid of mercy.

The head nun struck first, her movements fast and precise. Starr barely dodged the blade, countering with a punch that she blocked effortlessly. The two other nuns attacked in unison, forcing Starr to defend against multiple angles. He fought with everything he had, but they were skilled and ruthless.

The head nun slashed at him, and he felt the sting of the blade as it grazed his arm. Ignoring the pain, he kicked one of the nuns away and focused on the head nun. Their blades clashed, and Starr realized she was stronger than she looked. She pushed him back, and he stumbled, barely managing to stay on his feet.

Nadia screamed as one of the nuns grabbed her, trying to drag her away. Starr's heart beat with anger. He broke free from the head nun's assault and charged at the nun holding Nadia, tackling her to the ground and banging her head once against the cold marble floor. Nadia scrambled away.

Starr turned to face the head nun again, his breath coming in gasps. "This ends now," he said, his voice low and determined.

The head nun smiled, a cold, cruel smile. "Indeed, it does."

They clashed again, the fight intense and brutal. Starr's strength was waning, but he pushed through, driven by sheer determination. He landed a series of rapid blows to her face, each one weakening the head nun's defenses. Finally, he saw an opening and landed a haymaker right on her temple, knocking her out before she hit the ground.

The remaining nun hesitated, seeing their leader defeated. Starr took the opportunity and disarmed her, too, rendering her unconscious with a swift blow to the head.

Breathing heavily, he turned to Nadia. "Jesus Christ . . . are you okay?"

She nodded. "Oh my God, yes . . ."

He checked his watch. They had less than seven hours to make their pick-up point. He led her to the outer wall.

Scaling it quickly, they climbed into the shitty Russian car and disappeared into the night, leaving the convent and its dark secrets far behind.

Chapter Seventeen

The massive warship was more than 1,000 feet long, yet the storm was tossing it around in the ocean like a toy in a bathtub. Waves were crashing onto its decks, and the rain was coming down in torrents.

It was an aircraft carrier and a battleship, melded together into one almost fantastically sized weapon of war. It carried more than 100 warplanes—including many Americanized but Russian-built Su-34s, fierce, long-range fighter bombers. It also carried nine massive 16-inch guns, a vast array of anti-ship and anti-aircraft weapons, and down below, stored in its munitions locker, a handful of nuclear weapons.

Despite the terrible weather, the ship was launching a bunch of its warplanes, off to fight someone, somewhere, most likely someone who was an enemy of America or had attacked one of its allies. One of the many reasons why the USS *USA* was such a fearsome weapon is that its adversaries knew that, if they were after you, the people running it would not sleep until they got you. Doing carrier operations during a typhoon was almost routine to them.

Angel stood in the shadows of the rain-soaked flight deck, her large robe and hood protecting her from the tempest. She watched, unseen, as the Americanized-Su-34s were brought up from below decks and prepared for launching. Bombs attached, fuel sloshed in, the activity of the deck was almost magical between the sheets of rain.

Finally, the first Su-34 was setup for launch. She watched as the pilot climbed into the plane and started its engines. Its nose was connected to a steaming catapult. Its engines went to full scream. A deckhand gave the signal to the pilot to get ready to be fired off the flight deck.

That's when Angel stepped out of the shadows, just far enough for this particular pilot to see her.

"Be safe," she whispered to him.

A second later, the catapult was engaged, and the plane was rocketed off the ship and into the stormy night.

Chapter Eighteen

Near Demask

They were trapped.

Russian troops were all around them, and their fighter jets were overhead. In between, a flock of deadly suicide drones had been constantly circling their position, just waiting for a chance to kill them.

All thanks to a shitty Russian-made car.

Starr knew he shouldn't have been surprised. The beat-up, shot-up Lada Granta broke down just half a mile from the convent. Forced to leave it in a ditch, they found refuge in an abandoned farmhouse, right on the edge of the battlefield. A relic of better times, it was now a mere shell, its windows shattered, its walls pockmarked with bullet holes. Despite its condition, it provided sanctuary for them—and they needed it.

As soon as they'd reached the farmhouse, Starr heard the unmistakable whine of a Russian Shahed-131/136 drone overhead. Unlike the unarmed Zala recon drones which had been tracking them all night, the Shahed was a kamikaze drone, much louder, much more ominous. It was loaded with munitions and once it found its target, would crash into it with unfailing accuracy.

Three more showed up over the next four hours, the last one just ten minutes before. Now Starr checked his watch.

He couldn't believe it. They'd been trapped in the farmhouse for nearly five hours.

It was maddening.

They were less than a mile away from the pick-up point but with less than an hour to get there. True, there were Russians everywhere, but the real problem was, even if they did get out of the farmhouse alive somehow, some of the most violent combat since the end of World War II was raging in the no-man's land they had to cross. How did he ever expect them to do that?

Starr's military training had kept them alive to this point, but the constant tension was taking its toll. Nadia was surprisingly resilient but exhausted. When it was clear they wouldn't be going anywhere for a while, she lay down on the dirty floor and went to sleep. He moved over next to her and had been standing guard all this time.

He finally closed his eyes for a moment and wondered what Angel was doing at that exact moment.

He was wide awake in the next second, though.

Outside . . . something was different.

Suddenly he couldn't hear any of the commotion that had been going on non-stop since they began hiding in the farmhouse. No sounds of Russian tanks rumbling by; no more sounds of any jet fighters or drones overhead.

All was quiet . . .

It was so quiet, Nadia actually woke up and asked: "What's the matter?"

Starr's expression turned grim.

"Stay down," he told her, grabbing his M-4 and moving towards the window.

Through the broken glass, he saw the telltale navigation lights of a Mi-42 Hind helicopter approaching; it was bearing Russian markings. It was flying in a calm manner, not the aerial acrobatics you saw when an aircraft was flying close to the battle zone. For that moment, it was as if someone had stopped the war. Where had he heard *that* before?

Soldiers in green Spetsnaz uniforms were already jumping out of it. He watched as they set up a firing line, not twenty feet from the farmhouse.

"Damn . . ." he whispered urgently.

He hurried Nadia to the far corner of the room and shielded her with his body.

The barrage started just an instant later. Five soldiers were firing their AK-47 assault rifles point blank at the tiny house, tearing through wood and stone alike, filling the place with hundreds of bullet holes, smoke and the stink of cordite.

The barrage finally stopped. When Starr looked up, five Spetsnaz soldiers were standing over him. They were suited up with ammunition bandoleers and stylized masks over half their faces that made them look like human skeletons. Under their team patches, it said two words: *Rasstrelle Otryad*—Execution Squad. One of them, the biggest brute of all, was obviously the team leader,

Starr sized them up and knew starting any kind of a gunfight now would most definitely be fatal to Nadia and himself. So, they took his M4, his Glock, and all his ammunition. The team leader called someone on his radio and was soon talking in guttural Russian.

"We have the lollipop," he reported. "And a guy from NATO."

The reply was a barrage of rapid-fire Russian.

The gist of it was: "Take the girl, execute Mr. NATO . . ."

The Spetsnaz soldiers wasted no time. They went through a ghoulish exercise, picking lots for who would be the one to shoot Starr. Finally, one man "won" the honor. He was the youngest of the group.

Nadia started screaming once she realized what was going to happen. She clung to Starr, crying hysterically. But one of the soldiers roughly lifted her up and carried her out of the farmhouse. The rest of the Spetsnaz troops followed behind, except for the man who was to be Starr's executioner.

As he was going out the door, though, the team leader said: "Next time my boss sees Angel, I'll make sure he tells her how her boyfriend, the one who likes her to dress up like Supergirl, died like a coward, crying and begging for his life."

Now kneeling, his head forced down, his hands behind him grabbing the back of his boots, Starr was two seconds away from eternity.

Yet he still wondered: "How does he know Angel's name?"

Nadia was thrown onto the copter, placed on the floor, and surrounded by the soldiers. They waited until they heard the two shots, and then the last man came running out of the farmhouse, still masked, his helmet almost falling off his head. He jumped aboard, landing on the floor next to Nadia, who was still hysterical. His colleagues high-fived him and then the gunship finally took off.

Suddenly the squad leader was in Nadia's face.

"Listen, my dear," he shouted at her. "It's time you learned a valuable lesson if you're going to survive as a piece of candy. There are no more heroes left in this world. Do you know why? Because we just shot the last one. Now, there's only us bad guys left."

The Hind gunship did a long slow bank to the right, turning almost 360-degrees and heading back to the mansion, where it all began.

The flight took all of five minutes, then the copter set down on a helipad constructed on the roof of the mansion's main building.

Four soldiers climbed out first, the squad leader and three riflemen.

But when they turned to carry Nadia off the plane, they found themselves looking down the barrel of an AK-47 assault rifle.

Their young comrade—the man who'd killed the NATO representative—was now pointing his weapon at them.

The last thing they heard was Chris Starr saying: "Sorry boys, but you picked the wrong side of history."

Due to the noise of his rotor blades the Hind pilot had no idea what was going on just behind him.

Only when he felt the touch of cold steel on his cheek, pushing him to the left did he realize the Spetsnaz squad he'd been carrying were now all lying outside the copter, full of holes.

He turned right not to see a colleague but a complete stranger.

"Your other comrade decided to stay behind," the man said to him in a very distinctive American accent. "That's what happens when you're about to shoot someone in the head but don't know they have a switchblade in their boot. If you do it right, you can cut all the major tendons and arteries behind both their knees in just one motion. Bottom line, your friend back in the farmhouse is still alive but he's never going to dance again. But your comrades laying out there? Their dancing days are over.

"Now, here's your choice. Join them out there or fly us where we want to go."

The pilot looked back at him like he was crazy, which at this point, he was.

He realized the American was not only holding a pistol to his head, he was also displaying a very large switchblade . . . still dripping with blood. It was like a scene from a horror movie, which was exactly the point.

"I will take you anywhere you want to go," the pilot told him.

***

The Hind lifted off, but within seconds every weapon on the mansion's grounds opened up on it. Tracers lit up the night sky, and explosions rocked the gunship as the terrified pilot tried to maneuver through the barrage, knowing that it was his own men who were so suddenly trying to kill him. Starr was strapped into the copilot's seat. Nadia was right beside him, strapped into the flight engineer's jump seat, determined they would not get separated again.

As the Hind slowly rose into the night, the smoky expanse of the Ukrainian landscape stretched out before them. Starr checked his crappy watch. The pick-up time was in 19 minutes.

But disaster struck seconds later.

The Russian pilot was hyper-focused on evading the ground fire. The problem was, Hinds were notoriously slow climbers, so it was getting battered as it clawed for altitude. Its armor absorbed most of the hits, but it was a dangerous, high-anxiety ride. Still the pilot pushed the helicopter to its limits, zigzagging as best he could through the tracer-laden sky.

"Just a little longer," he told them. "Then we'll be out of the worst of it."

But time ran out for him, just an instant too soon.

One moment he was working the controls feverishly. The next, a single round from an AK-47 came through the cockpit glass, punctured his skull and killed him instantly.

Everything seemed to stand still. The helicopter's ascent, the explosions going on all around it. The night itself—just stopped.

Starr reached over and checked, but the man was clearly dead.

Now what?

Starr was not a helicopter guy. He'd flown just about everything else, but copters were a different kind of bird. Nevertheless, he pulled the dead pilot off the controls and took over himself. He knew the secret was to keep it level no matter what and he began working the controls to do just that.

He continued the slow climb, and they were indeed out of most of the ground fire within a few seconds. Miraculously he could see the monastery about a half mile ahead. And not too far from that was the CD building—and just a little beyond that, the small hill where he'd been dropped off and to which he had to return so he and the young girl could get out of this hell.

Pick-up time was in less than 15 minutes, but for the first time since he'd been dropped into this place, he had a glimmer of hope that he might fulfill the mission after all.

But suddenly, a warning light began to flash on the control panel. The needle on the fuel gauge was plummeting. Starr cursed under his breath. The Hind had been damaged more severely than he realized, and their fuel tanks had taken the brunt of it. They were running out of fuel fast. Desperation surged through him as he scanned for a place to land. Crashing was inevitable, but he needed to minimize the impact to keep Nadia safe.

Through the darkness, he spotted a dense patch of forest. It looked like nature's equivalent of a mattress factory, with thick, cushioned trees that might absorb some of the crash's force. He aimed for it, struggling to keep the Hind steady as it lost altitude. The ground rushed up to meet them. He put his arms around her and braced for impact.

The helicopter crashed through the canopy, branches snapping and tearing at the hull. The initial impact was brutal, but it stopped their momentum, so when they finally hit the ground, it was not as violent as it could have been. Starr was thrown against his harness, the air knocked out of him, but he never let go of Nadia.

When the dust settled, he checked her condition. Still wrapped in his arms, she was shaken but unhurt.

They climbed out of the wreckage, Starr wincing at the pain in his ribs. The forest was eerily silent, the crash's noise likely alerting any nearby forces. He knew they had to move quickly. The friendly Ukrainian lines were still a few hundred yards away, and the landscape between them was a treacherous battlefield. But they had no other choice. The pick-up time was now less than twelve minutes away.

"You know what to do?" Starr asked Nadia.

She actually laughed a little. "Yes— 'no matter what happens, stay close!'"

Starr led her through the dense underbrush. The forest provided cover, but it also slowed their progress. They navigated through the trees, constantly alert for any signs of danger. As they approached the edge of the forest, the sounds of war grew louder. They were entering a zone riddled with trenches and craters from relentless shelling.

Starr paused at the tree line, assessing the situation. The battlefield was a nightmare, a no-man's-land littered with obstacles. Trenches crisscrossed the area, and bursts of gunfire echoed in the distance. He turned to Nadia, seeing the determination in her eyes despite the fear.

"We need to move fast but stay low," Starr said. "And don't stop for anything."

They sprinted from the cover of the trees, darting into a nearby trench. The muddy walls provided some protection, but the air was thick with the smell of cordite and decay. Starr peered over the edge, mapping out their next move. They had to cross several open areas, each one a potential death trap.

He led the way, moving from trench to trench, always keeping Nadia close. They crawled through the mud, avoiding the watchful eyes of Russian soldiers all around them. At one point, they were forced to dive into a crater as six Russian soldiers passed dangerously close by. They held their breath, hearts beating loudly until the danger was gone.

Emerging from the crater, they continued their perilous journey. Each step brought them closer to safety, but the final stretch was the most dangerous. They had to cross an open field, exposed to anyone watching. Starr knew they had to make a break for it.

"On my signal, we run," he told Nadia. "Don't look back, just keep running."

He waited for a lull in the gunfire, then gave the signal. They sprinted across the field, adrenaline fueling their desperate dash. Bullets whizzed past them, and Starr felt a sharp stinging in his leg as one grazed him.

He pushed through the pain, focusing on the tree line ahead.

They reached the relative safety of the trees, collapsing to the ground, gasping for breath. Starr checked his wound; it was superficial, but painful. He tore a piece of his shirt and tied it around his leg to staunch the bleeding.

The night was alive with the sounds of war. Artillery shells whistled through the air, exploding with thunderous force in the distance. They ran out of the trees and back into the trenches. The ground shaking beneath their feet. His heart was beating out of his chest, adrenaline coursing through his veins. The girl stayed up with him, her scant nun-ish clothing offering little protection against the bitter cold and rough terrain. But she was doing it.

"Keep close," he kept whispering urgently. "We'll get through this."

The girl nodded, her face pale and frightened. She clung to Starr's hand as they moved quickly, ducking and weaving through the labyrinth of trenches as bullets whizzed past them. The gunfire was relentless and coming from all directions.

They came to an intersection of trenches and went right, in the direction of the pickup spot. A sudden explosion rocked the trench a moment later, sending a shower of dirt and debris raining down on them. Starr threw himself over the girl, shielding her from the worst of the blast. When the dust settled, he looked up to see Russian soldiers advancing through the smoke.

Starr pulled the girl to her feet, and they sprinted down the trench. He could hear the shouts of Russian soldiers, the rattle of gunfire, the screams of the wounded. A chorus of destruction.

They rounded a corner and came face to face with a Russian soldier. The man's eyes widened in surprise, but Starr reacted first, raising his AK-47 and firing a quick burst. The soldier crumpled to the ground, but a half dozen more were behind him. Starr pushed the girl down and prepared to challenge them, six against one. But suddenly the Russians were cut down by a murderous stream of fire going right over Starr's head.

Someone had saved them.

"Over here!" a voice called out from further down the trench. Starr turned to see a handful of Ukrainian militiamen behind them. One was gesturing frantically to them.

Starr checked his watch. Eight minutes to pick up.

He guided the girl towards the friendly soldiers. They reached the relative safety of a deeper section of the trench, where the Ukrainians were returning fire, to an unseen enemy that was only mere feet away. Starr quickly displayed his fake NATO card.

"We can't stay here long," one Ukrainian soldier said in broken English, his face grim.

Starr could only agree. "We need to find another way out," he said.

The soldier pointed to a spot at the end of the trench nearest them. "There's a tunnel over there that leads to the outskirts of the village. Use it to escape."

"We'll all go," Starr told him.

The soldier nodded, firing a burst from his rifle to keep the enemy at bay. "You and the girl go first," he said. "We'll cover you."

Starr took the girl's hand again and led her through the winding trench. The sounds of battle were deafening now, and again they had to duck and weave to avoid the relentless gunfire. The girl stumbled, her strength was waning, but Starr kept her moving, urging her on.

"We're almost there," he said, his voice steady despite the chaos. "Just a little further."

They reached the entrance to the tunnel, a narrow, dark passageway. Starr glanced back to see the Ukrainian militiamen holding the line, their faces set with determination.

"Go, go!" they shouted, waving them into the tunnel. "We'll be right behind you!"

An instant after that, an artillery shell hit the militiamen's position dead on. There was a huge explosion, the ground beneath their feet seeming to give way, that's how powerful it was.

Starr's heart sank. They died for us, just like that?

But then the smoke blew away and one by one five soldiers popped the heads back up.

Starr couldn't believe it. Neither could Nadia.

"They're alive!" she cried with joy.

The soldiers were smiling and waving frantically at them.

"Go!" they were shouting. "Go . . .

Starr guided her into the tunnel, the darkness swallowing them up. Five minutes to go. The sound of gunfire grew muffled as they moved deeper into the passage, the walls closing in around them. The girl's breathing was labored, but she kept moving.

They ran for what seemed a long time. Starr checked his swatch. Three minutes to go.

Suddenly, a bright flash lit up the tunnel, followed by a deafening roar. The ground shook violently, and Starr was thrown off his feet, crashing into the wall. The girl screamed, and he scrambled to his knees, reaching for her in the darkness.

"Are you okay?" he asked, his voice strained.

"I-I think so," she replied, her voice trembling.

Starr helped her to her feet, his ears ringing from the explosion. "We need to keep moving. Come on."

They pressed on, the tunnel winding and twisting beneath the village. Starr's thoughts raced as he tried to piece together what had caused the explosion. It wasn't artillery or a missile; it felt different, almost otherworldly.

As they neared the end of the tunnel, another bright flash illuminated the passage, followed by a strange humming sound. Starr peered around the corner, the light growing brighter.

"What is that?" the girl whispered, her voice filled with awe and fear.

"I don't know," Starr replied, gripping his rifle tightly. "Stay close."

They emerged from the tunnel into a small clearing on the outskirts of the village. The night sky was ablaze with light, and Starr looked up to see a massive object hovering above them. It was sleek and chrome-like, with bright lights radiating from its surface.

"Is that . . . a UFO?" the girl asked, her voice trembling.

"No, it's not," Starr replied, his voice a mix of relief and disbelief. "But they are here to rescue us . . ."

The balloon looked massive, its body glistening in the moonlight. It hovered silently, its lights scanning the ground below. Starr could see the outlines of sensors and cameras, all focused on their location.

The girl clung to his arm, her eyes wide with fear and wonder. "But how? How did they know we were here?"

Starr shook his head. "That's need to know . . ." he told her. "But we need to get to higher ground so they can see us."

They moved quickly, climbing up the side of the trench to the small rise overlooking the village. The spy balloon followed them, its lights focused on their every move.

As they reached the top of the rise, the balloon descended, its lights growing brighter. Starr could hear the faint whirr of its engines, a sound that seemed almost soothing in the chaos.

A hatch opened on the side of the balloon, and a jump ladder dropped down. Starr helped the girl up first, her hands trembling as she gripped the rungs. Once she was secure, he followed, his heart pulsing with each step. The ladder swayed slightly, but he climbed steadily, his eyes focused on the hatch above.

They reached the top, and a pair of hands reached out to help Nadia inside. Starr pulled himself through the hatch, collapsing onto the floor of the balloon. The girl was beside him, her chest heaving with exhaustion.

"Welcome aboard," a voice said, and Starr looked up to see a man in a flight suit, his face obscured by a helmet.

Starr nodded, his body trembling with relief.

"Thank you," he said, his voice hoarse. "Thank you for getting us out of there."

He paused a moment and then added: "But please tell your boss that he and I have to talk immediately..."

Chapter Nineteen

18 hours later

The lights of Catalina Island twinkled faintly on the horizon, a distant beacon of civilization against the vast, dark expanse of the Pacific.

Starr sat silently in the back of the Osprey as it hummed low over the waves, looking out the window at that now-mysterious island to the northeast.

"Here I am again," he thought. "Or at least I'm back in the neighborhood."

The return trip had been a long one. First to the DARPA base in Poland, then on to Ramstein AFB in Germany, followed by a C-17 to Chicago, then an F-15EX to Nellis AFB in Las Vegas, and finally, an Osprey ride to the isolated island of San Clemente, like Santa Catalina, located just off the coast of Los Angeles. Each leg of the journey had its own layer of security, a veil pulled tight around whatever Agent Conrad had in store for him.

He'd left Nadia in the care of DARPA personnel at Ramstein. She'd slept the entire ride out from Ukraine, right on the floor of the spy balloon where she landed once they'd been brought aboard. She tried to stay awake for the journey from Poland to Germany on a Navy-contracted P2012 medevac plane, but that didn't last long either. She slept on the seat next to him while he wrote out his preliminary report.

They were met on the tarmac at Ramstein by a Navy medical team, and that's when he transferred her custody to the DARPA representatives. The end happened so quickly that they didn't have time to say more than a brief goodbye. But as she was put into a service car, she broke away for a moment, ran back to him, gave him the quickest hug imaginable, and then bounced back into the car like a pro.

So much for saying kids these days are wimps.

San Clemente was no ordinary place; Starr knew that much. Just 20 miles southwest of Catalina, it was a highly secret, ironclad military reservation where Navy SEALs trained for missions they couldn't talk about, even to their families. Rumors of an entire mock city hidden somewhere on the island—a twisted Disneyland where soldiers rehearsed the art of urban warfare—swirled among those in the know. Even deeper down the rabbit hole were stories of experiments performed here that never saw the light of day. It was a ghost island in many ways.

The Osprey touched down on the deserted airstrip near the southern tip of the island. Starr's instincts told him that Agent Conrad had chosen this place for a reason. He'd seen a lot in his time with Naval Intelligence, but nothing could quite prepare him for the unpredictable world that Conrad and his fellow DARPA mad scientists inhabited. A world where every shadow hid a secret, and every step forward felt like a step into the unknown.

The aircraft's hatch opened, and Starr climbed out into the cool night air. The pilot told him his orders were to wait, to which Starr replied that he hoped he wouldn't be too long.

"I've got all night, sir," the pilot said with a casual nod.

About a hundred yards down the runway, Starr saw a sleek G-50 Gulfstream, painted all black, its lights blinking softly in the dark. This was Agent Conrad's plane, no doubt, and even from here, Starr could sense the quiet menace that seemed to surround it.

He walked up to the aircraft and stepped inside. The interior was not what he expected. It wasn't a luxurious private jet but rather a very compact command center, almost like a miniature AWACS plane. The walls were lined with monitors and consoles, the hum of electronics filling the plane with a constant, low buzz.

Starr was led into a private cabin by a silent, stone-faced operative. Inside, Conrad waited, seated behind a small desk. The man was a picture of calm, his expression betraying nothing as Starr took a seat opposite him. For a moment, neither spoke. The only sound was the soft purr of the jet's engines, a steady rhythm that seemed to sync with the plane's electronic hum.

Conrad finally broke the silence, his voice as cold as the steel that surrounded them. "So, Ukraine was interesting," he began, his eyes narrowing slightly as he studied Starr.

Starr shrugged, playing it cool. "Interesting enough. But I doubt you brought me all the way here for another debrief."

A faint smile tugged at the corner of Conrad's mouth. "No, I read your report and I've been briefed on how you handled things over there. Impressive work, Lieutenant Starr. But there are a couple more issues just as urgent that we need to discuss."

Starr leaned back; he saw this coming. "Viktor Robotov?"

Conrad's expression darkened slightly. "Yes. A man we've known about for some time, but he's been around even longer. Anytime anything on the planet has been close to going out of control, he's there, involved somehow, but very much under the radar. But then he turns into a ghost. He disappears off the world stage for long periods, and when he resurfaces, it's never in the same place. You don't hear his name mentioned too much, but he's haunted European intelligence agencies for years."

"Then why not send a cruise missile his way? A Christmas gift, if you will," Starr suggested.

Conrad didn't laugh. "It's not that simple," he replied. "Viktor is deeply embedded. He's connected in ways we're only beginning to understand, but there's so little we actually know about him, it's impossible to know how much of it is true."

He paused for a moment, Starr being a bit surprised this was the first topic of their conversation.

Conrad began again. "So, is there anything you can remember about his men? The way they conducted themselves? Or even how they communicated with him? Anything you can remember will be valuable."

Starr froze for a moment. There was something he'd left out of his report—on purpose. Back in the farmhouse, right before he was due to be executed, the Spetsnaz unit leader mentioned Viktor's name in the same sentence as Starr's very own Angel. This had been haunting his subconscious ever since. The burning question: While Viktor might know Angel through her modeling career, how did he know that she and Starr were a couple? They had gone to great lengths to keep their relationship secret; never mind the games they played in the bedroom.

Starr's blood ran cold but he felt compelled to tell Conrad the first half of the Russian's comment but keep quiet about the rest.

As he told the story, Conrad's face became a mask of concern, something Starr wasn't used to seeing. "The part that bothers me," he said once Starr had finished, "the only way Viktor could know her name is if someone close to you, someone with access, mentioned it."

Starr felt a knot tighten in his stomach. The idea that someone had betrayed him, that someone had fed Viktor information about Angel and himself, was more than he could bear.

But Agent Conrad had already moved on. He retrieved a manila envelope from the desk drawer.

"Issue number two," he said, handing the envelope to Starr.

It contained several dozen photographs, obviously shot from a high-flying aircraft or possibly a satellite. They showed the ASI compound on Catalina—the spy retreat that DARPA had "rescued" him from. But something was wrong. The place was empty. There were no signs of life in any of the photographs. The entire complex looked like it had been abandoned.

"Who exactly sent you to that place?" Conrad asked him.

Starr couldn't take his eyes off the photos. "My office in Washington. Where I get all my orders from."

"Well, you should show them those photos. They were taken yesterday, and it sure looks like the place closed up shop pretty quickly. Your bosses might find that a little odd."

"Odd doesn't even begin to explain it," Starr replied, totally baffled by all of it.

"That place is supposed to be a spa of sorts, correct? A place to go on R&R?" Conrad asked.

"That's what I was led to believe, yes," Starr said, his head still spinning.

"Did they give you any psychological tests?" Conrad asked. "Deep dives into whatever it is you have going on?"

Starr shook his head in disbelief. "They gave me a bunch of them," he replied gloomily.

Conrad just shrugged. "I'm not saying I have any idea what was going on there, but if I were you, I'd be on the lookout for, let's say, strange things happening inside your head for the next couple of weeks. Some of those tests can have long-lasting residual effects that they'll never tell you about . . ."

Starr looked up at him, a quizzical expression on his face.

Conrad quickly added, "That's just what I've heard in these types of situations."

But before Starr could press for more details, Conrad stood and looked out the plane's window next to his desk, seemingly signaling an end of the conversation.

But as Starr got up to leave, the DARPA officer started to say something, but then hesitated, his usual steely composure wavering. He remained by the window, the darkness outside mirroring some kind of heaviness. Sensing the shift, Starr stayed silent, watching as the man who was always in control was suddenly struggling with something deeper, more personal.

Conrad finally turned back to him, his eyes glistening with tears.

"Lieutenant Starr," he began, his voice unusually low, "I hope you realize I owe you a debt I can never repay."

Starr was caught off guard by the emotion in Conrad's voice. He could only nod. "I was just doing my job," he managed to say, though he knew it had been much more than that.

Conrad shook his head, taking a step closer. "No, Lieutenant. You saved my daughter's life. You did more than just your job. You gave me back my world."

Starr was genuinely surprised. He had always considered Conrad a fierce hard ass. This side of him was unexpected.

"Nadia is a good kid," Starr said, almost in a whisper. "She'll be okay . . ."

The words hung in the air between them, heavy with gratitude. For a moment, the two men stood in silence.

Then Conrad reached into his pocket and took out a laminated business card. It had a phone number on it, nothing else. He handed it to Starr along with a small, ultra-thin cell phone.

"Exactly two dozen people have had access to that number in the last fifty years," he said. "You're number twenty-five. If you ever require assistance, anytime, anywhere, call that number on that phone. And if you need us to, we'll come and get you."

Starr nodded slowly, feeling the gravity of what Conrad had entrusted him with.

"I'm just glad she's safe," he added quietly, the words almost lost in the low hum of the plane.

Conrad gave a small, almost imperceptible nod, his eyes clouded with emotion.

"That Osprey will take you anywhere you want to go," he said.

Then he turned away and retreated back into the shadows of the cabin.

Starr watched him go, the intensity of the moment still lingering in the air. The only two other times he'd seen Conrad, he'd been calm, collected, and always in control. But this was different. This was a father, raw and vulnerable, in a way Starr had never imagined a stiff like Conrad could be.

As he stepped back out onto the airstrip, the Osprey's engines roared to life, ready to take him away from this island of secrets. He climbed aboard, the weight of the encounter with Conrad still heavy on his shoulders. The plane lifted off, and as the island faded into the distance, Starr's mind was a whirl of thoughts and questions.

But suddenly, one question jumped ahead of the rest, a question he'd never thought of until now.

How did Conrad find his daughter on Chazter-Bate in the first place?

Part Three

Chapter Twenty

The Osprey's rotors cut through the thick, foggy night like a knife, the sound a low, throbbing hum that seeped into Starr's bones.

Catalina Island once again emerged from the darkness, a shadowy silhouette against an even blacker sea. His decision to return to this place felt like a dull ache, but something deep down was driving him. Conrad had said the Osprey would take him wherever he needed to go and despite every warning bell telling him not to do it, including the fact that he still hadn't called Angel, he was going here anyway.

Now the foggy island rushed up to meet them as the Osprey went down-throttle, its pilot silent and barely seen in the low-light of the cockpit. Starr had given him a precise landing spot. Close to the island's only airport, where many of the island's abundant golf carts were stored. Starr felt he would need more than his own two feet for this one. He might need a getaway car.

The rotor craft stopped in mid-air and then started to descend, its downdraft stirring up a cloud of dust that mixed with the fog. The familiar sight of the airport brought Starr an odd flicker of nostalgia. He'd been here just days ago, but everything looked different, and the vibe definitely felt different. Something big had changed in those 72 hours. It was like he was landing on another world.

They touched down a few moments later and Starr stepped out. The Osprey lifted off behind him, disappearing into the mist as if it had never been there. The golf cart rental hut stood empty; its doors wide open. He found one with the keys in the ignition, jumped in and turned it on. The engine coughed to life, and he floored it, the tiny vehicle lurching forward on the gravel path.

Catalina's noodle roads twisted and turned, winding through a landscape that felt more like a dream than reality. Shadows danced in the periphery of his vision, but he kept his eyes forward, focusing on the beam of the cart's headlights cutting through the mist. The island was surely different at night. Shadows moved in the corners of his vision, and the stars above seemed to pulse with an otherworldly light. The bison, those lumbering beasts that had seemed almost comical during the day, now looked like phantoms in the moon's glow, watching him with eyes that seemed like lasers in the dark, then vanish as he sped past.

But it was the silence that unnerved him the most—the silence and the creeping feeling that someone, or something, was watching him.

ASI's compound loomed ahead, its dark silhouette barely visible through the fog. One instinct he had listened to was not to have the Osprey land so close to this place; that was the real reason for stealing the cart. This was not the time for a grand entrance.

He slowed down, the engine's hum lowering to a soft growl as he approached the gigantic A-frame. The building's facade was like a monolith now, no lights to be seen, its windows black and impenetrable. Conrad had told him this place was deserted—and he was right. It looked like an amusement park that suddenly closed its doors.

But why?

He pulled out his trusty Glock and went through the front door. It creaked in protest, the sound echoing through the hollow corridors. This place, so alive just days before, looked like it had been abandoned for years. Dirt and dust everywhere, windows left open to the wind. Coffee cups sitting on the tables in front of the massive fireplace seemed frozen in time.

He walked the halls, looking in each room he came to, finding nothing.

He reached his old room, number 1313—but it was as if he'd never been there. Down to the rooms where he'd gone through the tests. All empty. The horrible room in the sub-basement called Viewing Box 6. The trash room where he saw the faux, discarded bodies of robots, including Ms. Kosmo-Bolo. They were all not just empty; they'd been abandoned. Like someone blew a whistle and everyone just left.

He started back up to the main floor but then just stopped. Why was he here? What exactly was he looking for? Proof that it wasn't all some crazy dream? Or a vision intentionally planted in his head?

He tried to search his consciousness for any clue left over that might tell him what exactly happened. What happened that ASI would simply disappear, leaving the place like a post-modern California ghost town.

But nothing came through, though his mind wasn't blank. It was quite cloudy, almost stormy, not from the lack of information floating around him, but from too much of it.

And then, it began—the whispering. At first, it was a low murmur, a sound so soft it could have been mistaken for the wind, but Starr knew better. He'd heard these voices before—in the darkest corners of his mind, in the blackest hours of the night. The dead were speaking to him again.

He began walking quickly back towards the main entrance, the voices swirling around him, a chaotic symphony of despair and pain. Suddenly they were everywhere, echoing off the walls, bouncing off the floors, seeping into his brain. The weight of it pressed down on him like an anvil, the air around him growing thicker with every step. It was like hearing a hundred radio stations all at once, all with their volume turned up to the max. It was like he was going to drown in the sound.

"Enough!" he suddenly shouted, surprising himself with his ragged and desperate rasp.

But the voices only grew louder, their tone more frantic, more insistent. They clawed at his sanity, pulling him deeper into the abyss.

He could go no further. He stopped, sat against the dark wall and tried to will them away.

And then, suddenly, the voices stopped. But then a new sound echoed through the halls. Footsteps, steady and deliberate. He wasn't alone. The fog in his mind lifted just enough for him to turn, to face the shadow moving toward him.

"Lieutenant Starr?"

The voice was clear, cutting through the fog like a knife. It was familiar, maybe too familiar. She stepped into the light, her figure sharp against the darkness.

It was Maura McCann.

She was in her mid-20s, five-four, with dark red hair and incredibly bright blue eyes—they were almost neon. She was a member of the Republic of Ireland Special Detective Squad and she and he had some very strange adventures together in the past year or so, the last one bordering on mind-blowing.

He jumped up and locked her in a tight embrace.

"Maura?" He could barely get the words out, his throat dry and tight. "What are you doing here?"

"I could ask you the same thing," she replied. "How did you find me?"

He tried to focus, to pull the fragments of his thoughts together. "I didn't . . . I mean, I wasn't looking for you." His eyes narrowed as he tried to make sense of it all. "Why are you here?"

"I was here, at ASI, last week . . ." she said, as if it were the most natural thing in the world.

He was shocked. "I was here at the same time," he told her excitedly.

"I guess that doesn't surprise me too much," she replied.

She was dressed oddly. Gone was her usual Celtic hot cop get up of tight sweater, short skirt and black tights. Now she was dressed like a mom from Los Angeles who was visiting Catalina for the first time. Blousy blouse, capri pants and wedgy sandals. It was an odd ensemble, but she looked good in everything.

"They put me through all kinds of grotesque tests," she replied. "This after they said I was coming here as a guest of the American government, for a weekend retreat."

"They said the same to me," Starr replied. "They told me they were going to drill deep down to see why I have this ESP thing going on. But what they really did was probe my memory to see if I knew anything about . . . you know . . ."

He let the sentence hang there.

She pushed her flowing red hair back and moved closer to him.

"The God Satellite?" she asked.

Those words landed like a bomb on top of Starr's head.

"Yes . . ." he said. "The God Satellite . . ."

That was the name of the highly advanced and highly enigmatic piece of technology that he'd seen the image of during one of his painful sessions at ASI. Maura was the one who dubbed it the "God Satellite" after she coined the name from the acronym "Geospatial Observational Data," reflecting the satellite's ability to observe and collect vast amounts of information. But it was also equipped with incredibly advanced artificial intelligence, making it capable of performing tasks that seemed almost divine in scope. So, the name really applied.

But again, this thing was so deeply classified, it was at the bottom of a near-bottomless rabbit hole.

They'd tracked the very few people who knew about the strange satellite to a Vatican-owned observatory in Arizona. But once they got inside, most of what they'd heard and seen wound up being wiped from their memories. Both of them had a bad blank block in their prefrontal cortex. It's like they were there but they weren't.

"I think what they were trying to do," she told him. "was recover those memories of whatever happened to us back then."

"So, how did you get out of here?" he asked her.

"When it got to be way too much for me, I stole their air taxi," she said, with a devilish smile.

"You're the one?" he gasped remembering back to the commotion in the parking lot right before he left.

"I am," she said. "But something . . . something called me back."

She glanced around, her expression unreadable. "I guess I wasn't done here."

Starr shook his head, trying to clear the last vestiges of the dead voices from his mind. "Me, too," he said.

"So dramatic," she said, but with no humor—just a weary acceptance of the bizarre situation they found themselves in.

They walked out together, holding hands, staying close. He had left the A-Frame's huge doors open and now the fog was sweeping into the large empty lobby.

They stepped out into the stillness of the night, leaving the ASI compound behind them in the gloom. The air was thick with anticipation, each shadow a lurking threat, every rustle in the underbrush a reminder of the uncertainty they sensed around them.

"So, is everything they told us a lie here?" Maura's voice sliced through the heavy silence, tinged with frustration and disbelief. "And did they go through all this—just for us?"

Starr's mind churned, trying to assemble the disjointed pieces of the truth they'd been handed. The notion that they might be mere pawns in a larger, shadowy game gnawed at him. The people they'd interacted with—those who weren't robots—were they actors? Was this all part of some elaborate, twisted deception?

Then, another even more unsettling realization crept into his thoughts.

"If this was all fake," he murmured, almost to himself, "did they tell me the truth about the UFO movie set?"

Maura stopped in her tracks, her sharp eyes narrowing with suspicion. "What are you talking about?"

Starr recounted that when he was flying to ASI in the air taxi, they passed over what he thought was a movie set. He had a brief exchange with the drone's robot pilot who led him to believe that the strange site he'd seen below—a supposed crashed-UFO movie set—was just one of many productions filmed on the island. Starr's guide at the ASI itself assured him of the same thing. A movie about a crashed alien spacecraft was being made on the island.

But now, with everything else crumbling around them, Starr couldn't shake the feeling that what he saw was something a lot different.

"If they lied about everything else," he concluded, "then why would they be telling the truth about that?"

Maura's eyes flickered with a mix of recognition and shared understanding. The insanity of their situation was becoming clearer with every moment.

"Only one way to find out," she said.

Starr led the way to the waiting golf cart, and they sped off into the fog-draped night. The mist clung to them like a shroud, the shadows seeming to dance closer, as if drawn to their urgency. Above, the stars flickered like dying embers, casting a dim, otherworldly glow over the landscape, which now felt more foreign with each twist and turn of the road.

They arrived at a knoll overlooking a small valley—the place Starr had previously identified as the movie set. But now it was just a gaping wound in the earth, devoid of the bustling activity he'd seen before.

"Did they finish the movie?" Maura wondered aloud; her voice tinged with doubt. "Or did they retrieve the wreckage?"

Starr's gaze swept over the scene, his mind focusing with an intensity that blurred the edges of reality. His head throbbed—a familiar pain that came with the territory. His STPA-2 ability wasn't just about recalling events; it allowed him to visualize and manipulate them in great detail, as if he had a video playback in his mind. His Navy shrinks had likened it to having a mental DVR, something he could rewind, fast-forward, and even freeze-frame at will.

All he had to do was close his eyes, call up the recent past, and it would play out for him, just like on a big TV screen.

So, he went back to that moment a few days ago when he was in the air taxi, flying over this part of the island. The air cab had slowed to about 80 knots, giving him an unfettered view of the ground below. What he saw in those few seconds —a disc-shaped object, maybe fifty feet across, crumpled and stuck inside an outcrop of rock and sand. Wisps of smoke rose from it, and people in military camouflage had it surrounded. A dozen or more vehicles were about, and banks of high-intensity lights were also in the area.

But what did he really see? Slowing it down in his head, Starr noticed the absence of any stagehands, extras, or assistants running around the set. Instead, he saw people wielding hand excavators, jackhammers, and even picks and shovels, desperately digging into the massive mound. And yes, there were cameras on hand, but they were documenting the scene, not filming a scripted movie. And these people doing the digging weren't acting—they were desperately trying to unearth something buried deep in the ground. The tension on their faces was genuine.

The final reason he knew this was no movie set: there were no Teamsters around. That was the best proof of any.

"This wasn't anything to do with Hollywood," Starr whispered, the cold realization washing over him. "I'm sure of it now."

Maura watched him closely, her expression guarded, yet there was a flicker of belief in her eyes—or perhaps resignation to the madness that had become their reality.

"What now?" she asked, her voice steady despite the turmoil they both felt.

Starr didn't answer immediately. Instead, he reached into his coat and pulled out the laminated card and the encrypted cell-phone Conrad had given him. His hands shook slightly as he punched in the number, holding the phone to his ear.

The line clicked, and Conrad's voice came through, smooth and steady, like a lifeline in the storm.

"Lieutenant Starr?" Conrad asked, his tone all business. "Do you have a situation?"

"More of a question," Starr replied, his words spilling out in a rush. He recounted what he had seen at the crash site, the images replaying in his mind even as he spoke. When he finished, he asked: "Was this a DARPA aircraft?"

There was a long, heavy silence on the other end.

"It's not one of ours," Conrad finally said, his voice carrying a note of finality. "Beyond that, I don't know what to tell you. In the meantime, I believe your ride is there."

The sound of approaching rotors broke the silence. Starr and Maura looked up as the Osprey descended, its dark shape cutting through the mist. The wind whipped around them as they climbed aboard. The rotor craft took off and headed east, back towards the mainland, Catalina quickly receding into the fog behind them.

Inside the aircraft, the atmosphere was heavy, weighted down by everything left unsaid. Starr and Maura rode side by side, bodies pressed up against each other again, but not talking, just trying to figure it all out.

It was a quick ride. Maura had instructed the pilot to land in an empty field just a few miles from the San Diego airport. Then she texted an Uber to meet her there.

"I feel it's not wise to be seen together too much," she said to Starr. "Not until we know what was going on here."

"I agree," he said, but with an unexpected tinge of sadness. He really didn't want her to go.

The Osprey landed. Maura turned back to Starr; her expression softened by the shadows.

"I guess this is goodbye," she said, her voice low, almost lost in the drone of the engines.

"For now," he was just barely able to say.

"You really feel that way?" she asked him.

But before he could respond, she leaned in, and kissed him, her lips brushing against his with a tenderness that caught him off guard. He returned the kiss, but it was brief, fleeting, like a promise unkept.

She pulled away, her eyes lingering on his for just a moment before she turned and climbed off the Osprey.

Her Uber waited in the darkness, its headlights cutting through the night. She climbed in, and Starr watched as the car drove off, her silhouette fading into the fog, taking her back to Ireland and out of his life—at least for now.

Chapter Twenty-One

Something was wrong with Angel.

Starr could feel it. And it was crushing the very life out of him.

The soft glow of the setting sun filtered through the large bedroom windows now, casting long shadows against the wall. He sat on the edge of the bed, as always, his mind overloaded by the scariest aspects of his job. Too many strange missions, too many secrets, too many brushes with death lately. Each one bothered him in its own way.

But now, something else was gnawing at him: an inexplicable melancholy he felt whenever Angel was near. She was in the adjacent room now; her footsteps barely audible on the plush carpet. But even still he could feel it. The silence. The sadness. The hush.

They'd never been this quiet with each other before.

Their long-awaited reunion had been tearful, as Starr knew it would be, but not for the reasons he'd imagined. She met him at the pier in Dana Point, just as she said she would, but she wasn't wearing her Supergirl outfit. They hugged and it was emotional, but the tears were all hers. She apologized for the missed phone calls, and he apologized for not trying her on the Tomato Can sooner, but there was a deeper sadness there.

As they drove back to San Diego, he recounted everything that had happened since they'd last seen each other. She listened, astonished at all the right parts, but the tears never really stopped. Quiet, almost imperceptible, but they were there the whole way. When he asked what was wrong, her answer was always the same: "I'm just glad you're back. I was really worried about you."

But nothing changed once they got home. The heart-wrenching distance remained between them.

He glanced out the window at the lights of the city far below, trying to steady his thoughts. The world outside was so vast, so normal, yet his world had become a labyrinth of mysteries, each more confounding than the last. And now this?

What happens next? he thought.

The door to the bedroom creaked open, and he turned to see Angel standing in the doorway, her face partially obscured by shadows.

"Chris," she said softly, stepping into the room, now wearing a long, flowing white gown that brushed the floor. "We have to talk . . ."

Her voice carried an unusual weight, something that made his heart jump. She walked over to him, her gaze intense, and sat down beside him on the bed. For a long moment, she said nothing, simply staring into his eyes as if searching for something—some sign that he was ready for what she was about to say.

"You know I love you, right?" she began, her voice trembling slightly. Starr nodded, unable to find his own. "And I've always been honest with you . . . about almost everything."

"Almost?" Starr finally managed, his voice coming out more strained than he intended.

Angel took a deep breath, her eyes moist. "Chris, there's something I've been keeping from you. Something . . . huge. It's not just about me—it's about us, about everything."

Starr's stomach tightened. He reached out, taking her hand in his. "You can tell me anything," he said, though even as he said the words, he wasn't sure he wanted to know what was coming next. Had the videotape they'd shown him at ASI—her with another guy—been . . . real?

She closed her eyes for a moment, gathered her thoughts, then opened them again.

"Chris . . . I'm not who you think I am," she said. "I'm . . . I'm not just a model or a girl with a love for adventure. I'm something else, something . . . more."

"What are you saying?" Starr asked, his voice barely above a whisper.

She hesitated for another moment, but then finally it just came out.

"I'm an angel," she said, her words hanging in the air like a profound truth. "A real one."

Starr blinked, the words not fully registering at first. "What? An angel?"

She nodded slowly, tears starting to stream down her cheeks again.

"But angels aren't real," he heard himself say, suddenly concerned that the woman he loved more than anything was having a mental breakdown. "That sounds a little crazy, honey . . ."

Angel nearly collapsed when he said this. So, he was almost floored by her next question...

"Does this mean we're over?" she asked tearfully. "That you don't love me anymore because I'm a freak?"

His heart dropped. As strange as all this was, he knew he'd devastated her. He immediately embraced her.

"That would never happen," he said. "In this world or any other."

She took a deep breath and seemed relieved.

"But, Angel, honey," he said, his mind pleading for something to make sense, "please tell me what's going on."

They got closer together on the bed.

"I've been sent here to protect you, to watch over you," she told him, her eyes still watering but now with sincerity. "But there's more to it than that. I've also been watching over someone else too, someone in a different . . . place."

"Someone else in this building?" he asked urgently.

She actually laughed. "No, silly," she replied. "Someone not from this place. This dimension. This universe. I'm not even sure what the difference is myself."

For Starr, it was getting more absurd, more impossible . . .

Yet the earnestness in her eyes, the trembling in her voice—it was clear she wasn't joking. But he didn't know what to say, how to respond to something so fantastical.

"This person's name is Hawk Hunter," Angel went on, her voice barely steady. "He's a fighter pilot, on an aircraft carrier, but not in our world. He's in a parallel universe, let's call it—a place where the rules are different, and where the battles are . . . unimaginable."

Starr stared back at her, his heart still pounding in his chest.

"You've been protecting him? In another . . . universe?"

"Yes," Angel whispered. "I've been acting as his guardian angel, guiding him through battles, helping him survive. It's . . . it's hard to explain, but I'm connected to him, just as I'm connected to you. I can't fully control it, but I feel everything he goes through—every danger, every fear. We are entangled in a way, but he doesn't even really know it."

Starr continued staring into her eyes, searching for some sign that this was all just a bad dream, that he'd wake up and everything would be normal again. But all he found was the woman he loved, and what she was telling him sounded absolutely insane.

She paused, looking away as if lost in the memories of another world. "Hawk's been through so much, Chris. He's fought in wars you can't even imagine. In his world, the battles are beyond anything we've faced. And he's just about the only one who can stop them."

She reached out, cupping his face in her hands. "Chris, I love you more than anything. But you need to understand that my being here, my love for you—it's part of something bigger. Something that transcends our understanding of reality."

Her eyes were suddenly shining with a light that seemed almost otherworldly.

"And I know it sounds crazy," she went on, "but there's more. Hawk's battles aren't just confined to his world. They're bleeding into ours. The forces he's fighting—they're trying to break through, to invade our reality. And I'm afraid that if we don't do something soon, both our worlds could be destroyed."

Starr felt a deep, overwhelming fear settle in his chest. The woman he loved, the person he trusted more than anyone, was telling him something so unbelievable, so terrifying, that he didn't know how to react. But one thing was clear—she believed it. Every word.

He just shook his head. "I just don't know what to say, honey. What you're telling me sounds like a really bad science fiction plot. Is there anything you can show me that would convince me this is all . . . real?"

It was almost as if she'd been waiting for him to say just that.

"Let me try," she replied, deadly serious now.

She stood up, took a few steps back, slowly raised her arms—and suddenly, she had wings.

Big, white, fluffy wings. Just like those you'd see on a holy card, in a religious painting, or in a movie.

He nearly passed out, he was so startled. At first, he thought she was playing a joke on him, that this was part of some bizarre outfit she was modeling or something.

But in the next moment, he knew this was no joke. These wings were real, organic. They moved when she moved. She took a breath, they rose; she exhaled, they relaxed. And when she put her arms down, they folded back behind her. Once again, he almost lost it. He'd seen some pretty messed-up things in his life, but nothing like this.

"But angels aren't real," he insisted, grasping at reason. "I mean, not the way we imagine them to be. They only showed up in paintings way back when? The Fourth Century, maybe? They're a creation of humans. And they only had wings because they were said to be messengers, and could fly down from Heaven and . . ."

His words trailed off. Now he felt like he was in a movie—a very bad one.

She let a few seconds pass, then she said: "And do you know who this Hawk Hunter guy is fighting in his parallel world?"

Starr could only numbly shake his head no.

She leaned over and whispered in his ear: "Viktor Robotov."

Chapter Twenty-Two

Five minutes later, Starr was in his own apartment, having gone through the worm hole at Angel's urging.

He was trembling now. All over. His reality had just been thrown for a loop. He had arrived at one conclusion earlier—that after listening to Angel's fantastic story, either she was having psychological issues—or he was.

But hearing the name Viktor Robotov changed all that.

As crazy as it sounded, mentioning his name made this fantastic thing just a little less fantastic. How would Angel know Viktor's name, especially if DARPA was just now finding out about him? Maybe there was a one in a trillion chance she heard it thrown out at one of the many cocktail parties she attended in the course of her modeling gigs.

But how did the Spetsnaz unit leader know that *she* was *his* girlfriend, and that Viktor knew who *she* was? Again, maybe somewhere along the way, Viktor saw one of her covers and fell for her, like a lot of guys did under the same circumstances. But then how could she mix him up in all this trans-dimensional, multi verse thing?

But it was something else she told him that made him make the leap. That's why he was sitting in his apartment, dressed in his Navy-issued foul weather gear, from boots to his arctic-certified hoodie, waiting for her to summon him back into his place and receive "the surprise of his life."

The tipping point? Before temporarily exiling him, she'd said: "My God, Chris. These people even have Tomato Cans."

Now with that bouncing around in his head, along with Angel's statement that they both were all somehow mixed up in this, another thought shook him. What if what Conrad warned him about—that the deep dive psychological tests they'd given him at the mysterious ASI compound had some kind of lingering effects and all this high strangeness was just a result of that?

She called for him an instant later.

He went through the wormhole. It was a bit of a chore, trying to contract himself with all his arctic gear on. He came out of her closet to see her standing in the middle of the bedroom, wearing a long dark robe with a giant hood. She had the hood up and it almost shrouded her face.

They looked like they were going to a really bad Halloween party.

She motioned him over. He started to say: "You know, I had a battery of psych tests when I was on Catalina, and they might be affecting my judgment here and . . ."

That's as far as he got.

Flash!

The next thing he knew he was standing on a high cliff, looking down at a vast ocean. The sky was overcast, and the wind was blowing fiercely. In his last rational instant, he thought he was glad he'd worn his foul weather gear.

They were atop a cliff on the northern side of Santa Cruz de Flores, the westernmost island of the Azores chain. Angel was standing beside him, but strangely the winds were not blowing her clothes around; it seemed like the elements had no effect on her at all. Starr kept frisking himself up and down just checking that he was actually here. This was not his reality. This was more like being in a dream. But it was happening at the same time. Or at least he thought it was.

Angel pointed towards the east. It took him a moment to focus his eyes, but then he saw what she was indicating. It was a fleet of some kind. Warships, certainly. But of the strangest kind.

There was an enormous aircraft carrier in the lead. It was flanked by what looked like heavily armed seagoing tugboats, eight of them, two of them under tow.

Behind them were five of the strangest ships he'd ever seen, because they weren't really ships at all. They were airplanes that operated like warships, sailing on a cushion of air that lifted them about ten feet above the surface of the ocean. They called them Ekranoplans and in his world they rarely worked, rarely flew and all wound up as heaps in Russian junk yards somewhere.

But possibly the strangest thing of all, as the strange armada approached, Starr could see several squadrons of Russian-made Su-34 fighters bombers lined up on the deck of the carrier—but with American-style red, white and blue markings on them. Indeed, one of the largest U.S. flags Starr could remember seeing was flying off the mast of this gigantic warship.

Behind the Americanized Russian warplanes was a group of Yak-28s, Russian-made jump jets that probably had the worst reputation of any aircraft of the Cold War and beyond.

One last surprise, hanging off the back of the carrier's enormous deck were two AC-130 gunships, just like used by the U.S. special ops back . . . well, back where he was from.

But these planes were painted oddly and looked to have three or four times the number of guns sticking out of them.

For the first time Angel spoke to him.

"There they are," she said, with a touch of admiration in her voice. "They call themselves the United Americans, but they trace their roots back to 1987 or so when in this world, there was a nuclear war between the U.S. and Russia—literally World War III—which Russia won because our Vice President was quisling. These people, well, they just hung on by their fingernails, kept fighting to keep the idea of a real America alive until they grew and grew into the most feared and respected military in this strange, strange world."

"And those guys really have Tomato Cans?" he asked.

She looked over at him and said: "Yes, they do . . . but there's more. I want you to see how dedicated and heroic these people are. And to do that, you've got to meet Hawk Hunter."

Flash!

Suddenly Starr was sitting at a bar in what appeared to be an English pub but with a lot of Scandinavian trappings. Vikings' helmets, large steel mugs. Reindeer horns above the fireplace.

It was night-time. Angel was behind the bar, serving drinks. She was now dressed in her usual hang-around clothes: plaid shirt, jeans & a white baseball cap. She was also wearing an apron.

She served him a beer and then whispered: "OK, pay attention here . . ."

She went outside for a moment and came in with a guy who looked like a rock star if rock stars wore crash helmets and flew jet fighters.

He had the hair; he had the build, and he had that self-effacing vibe many rock idols had.

Who the hell is this? he thought.

He had his answer a moment later . . .

As soon as the bar's clientele saw him, he was mobbed—just like a rock star. Everyone in the place wanted to hug him, kiss him—men, women, even few kids. The crowd dragged him to a table just off the bar, the best seat in the house. He was quickly surrounded, with many people crowding in close to him. Many even reached out to touch his hair.

Starr turned to the old timer next to him and asked: "Who is that guy?"

The old timer looked at him like he was from Mars.

"Who is he?" he asked him. "That's Hawk Hunter, my friend. They call him the Wingman. He's the best fighter pilot who's ever lived."

The old guy's eyes lit up as he picked up his beer to join the crowd.

"We don't get many visitors on our little island," he said. "And this guy's a real-life celebrity . . ."

Flash!

Suddenly Starr was standing on a snowy and very cold airfield. It was daytime and there were lots of people around him. In front of them was one of the weird Americanized Russian Su-34 fighter bombers. It sported a variation of the USAF markings but was also pimped out like a hot rod. The blue and white paint job was wild and exquisite.

Angel was beside him. She was wearing a winter parka; the hood was down, and she had her white baseball cap on. There was no mistaking her, curls fluttering in slow motion despite the brisk wind.

The man who she had just ushered into the bar—otherworldly hero Hawk Hunter—was now sitting in this large warplane, obviously getting ready to take-off.

Starr was a little amazed at all this. In this universe, rock stars *do* fly jet fighters, he thought. Interesting . . .

The crowd was obviously here to give him a hearty, if tearful send off. Angel leaned over and told Starr Hunter's warplane had been forced down here about a week before and while awaiting parts, he'd saved the little island from some nasty Russians stationed on the next island over.

"That's the kind of guy he is," she said. "These people are survivors from World War III. We're out in the middle of the North Sea for God's sake, closer to

Scandinavia than England. Yet even here, he lent a helping hand."

But now Hunter was leaving, and it was quite clear that none of the islanders wanted to see him go. They were waving flags and shouting goodbye as he increased his throttles, preparing for an imminent launch. The rock star pilot waved back to them. Starr could see him taking extra gulps from his oxygen mask, as if he was trying to center his emotions. Then he brought his engines up to full power and got ready to pop the brakes.

Then he glanced back at the crowd one more time—and that's when he saw Angel.

He looked right at her. Like laser beams going back and forth. Angel blew him a kiss, surprising Starr.

An instant later, his afterburners kicked in.

And then he was gone.

Flash!

Suddenly Starr was standing atop a building in the middle of Hamburg, Germany. It was the Atlantic House, the tallest building in the city. It was nighttime, date unknown. Starr took in the surroundings and thought this might be Hamburg as it looked back in the late 80s or 1990s, but it was certainly different. First, about half the neon signage across the city was in Russian. And a large part of the downtown was separated and cordoned off. A Russian enclave perhaps?

But it was still very much a seaport town even though its inner harbor and the Elbe River beyond was full of Russian warships.

Before he could ask the question, Angel told him: "Remember, in this place, Russia won World War III."

She put her hand up to her ear and added: "Now listen..."

Starr strained to hear something above the normal sounds of a busy, bustling city at night. There was nothing at first, but then he heard them coming. It was a combination of a high-pitched whine and a deep throaty roar. Starr knew that sound. Cruise missiles. Lots of them.

They started falling onto the city; as soon as the first one impacted, the city's air raid sirens began blaring. They were landing three or four at a time down near the city's docks, hitting oil storage facilities located there. He heard targets blowing up around him, some of them individual sites that he could only imagine were air-defense positions. Soon after that, Russian-made fighter planes were falling out of the sky in ones and twos.

Another wave of cruise missiles followed the first and most of these missiles landed on Hamburg's huge airport, rendering it unusable in seconds. As a coup de grace, a third wave hit the city's *Nikolaifleet,* the largest canal in a city of canals. It unleashed a tidal wave of water that raced through the streets of downtown, ravaging buildings to military vehicles and everything in between.

Suddenly the entire city was either alight with uncontrollable fires or drowning in a flood of seawater. Starr was just waiting for a rain of frogs and swarms of locusts to appear.

And then there was a new noise. Russian fighters had already taken to the skies before their base at the Hamburg Airport had been blown into oblivion, and they were now crashing at an alarming rate. Starr turned to his right and saw a single Russian Su-34 flying just 100 feet above the *Reeperbahn*. It took a sudden right turn and incredibly landed on a small rectangular island in the Kraftwerk Canal close to where the city's oil refineries were burning fiercely.

As he watched, three men scrambled out of the jet and got into an inflated rubber raft. With great strength and courage, they started motoring toward the nearest land; a spit sticking out into the Elbe.

"What is going on here?" Starr finally had to ask. It was as if he was watching some kind of real action movie. "Who are those guys?"

"That's Hawk Hunter and two of his men," Angel explained. "And that spit of land houses a notorious detention center, called *Das Blutgefangnis,* the Blood

Prison. A colleague of theirs is locked up there and at this very moment he is being tortured to death."

"And . . .?" he asked.

"And they're here to rescue him," she replied.

Starr was a little baffled. "They did all this?" he asked. "For one person?"

She looked at him and nodded slowly. "That's how these people are . . ."

She explained that it took great coordination and skill to pull off such an audacious act. It involved a massive submarine, the massive aircraft carrier and many warplanes flying in bad weather at night all in an effort to make this thing go smoothy.

"The person most responsible for this is Hawk," she said. "He's considered the best fighter pilot in the world—or in this world at least. And he's great at leading missions like this. He has ESP just like you, in fact you two are a lot alike. Maybe that's not a coincidence that he's the person I'm here to help when he needs it."

More explosions rocked the city. The fire down on the oil docks was raging totally out of control. The city itself was in the throes of a mass panic.

He felt Angel tug on his arm. "And he needs my help right now."

Flash!

Suddenly, Starr was in complete darkness.

He let his eyes adjust to the murk. He was in a passageway, made of stone, very dark, barely lit. It smelled of dampness and mold. Only one word came to him: dungeon.

Angel was standing next to him, but he was much deeper into the shadows. She was wearing her long black cloak and hood, again looking like something from a ghost movie.

Suddenly someone was running down the sloping tunnel towards them. He came around the corner and Starr was able to see him up close. It was Hawk Hunter, the rock-star pilot, long hair, flight suit, handsome, determined looking but also looking a little lost. He didn't know which way to go.

Suddenly Angel stepped out of the shadows. She pointed to the middle hallway. She urgently whispered to him: "That way. Go—that way."

Starr could hear voices shouting, and gunshots pinging off walls nearby. The fog was building, and if anything, the lights were getting dimmer.

But Hunter stopped in his tracks.

"Who are you?" he asked Angel.

She pulled back the hood just enough to reveal her face. She looked at him—and smiled.

But what was really strange was he didn't seem to recognize her—at first. So, she pulled the hood all the way back to reveal that she was wearing a white baseball cap underneath.

That's when it hit him.

Hunter looked so shocked he seemed frozen to the spot.

She just shook her head, strawberry blonde curls swaying this way and that, and laughed at his reaction.

"Are you . . . an angel or something?" he asked her.

Angel gave him a look and said: "Do you really want to know?"

But she didn't wait for him to reply.

She commanded him: "Get your friends and go! Take the middle hallway—hurry!"

Flash!

Suddenly, Starr was in the war room of an aircraft carrier.

He was standing at the back of a crowd of very concerned officers huddled around the carrier's communications console. All eyes were fixed on the room's huge TV screen. And sure enough, next to the screen were two Tomato Cans.

The screen was showing a wave of unsophisticated but dangerous-looking drones heading right for the carrier's broadside.

One of the men studying the screen said: "They're one minute away."

Starr was wondering if he heard that right. He felt Angel's hand touch his briefly. She looked at him and whispered: "Watch what happens . . . This is how lucky they are."

One man was sitting at the center of the communications console, his fingers madly pushing two different lighted panels with lightning speed. With each push, he was listening in on a separate radio frequency, rejecting it for some reason, before moving on to the next one.

It seemed like the problem was the enemy used very unusual radio frequencies to communicate with its flying robots. And because there were hundreds of possible channels that the drones could be tuned to, the only way to find out was to listen in on all of them until he hit upon the one he was looking for.

But everyone in the war room, including Starr, knew they were looking at a disaster here. Then came an ominous warning from one of their picket ships that these drones were carrying even larger bombs than thought before. The next thing they heard, the picket ships were shooting at the drones as they were going over their heads. Then communications with the pickets went dead.

The seconds continued ticking away. The man's fingers continued moving at high speed, but the swarm would be here in less than a minute. The officer who appeared to be in command of the aircraft carrier called for the ship's company to open fire on the drones. It was going to be one, gigantic barrage, fired in very close.

It sounded like a single, overwhelming, ear-splitting bang! as all of the carrier's heavy guns fired at once. The result, played out in color on the big TV screen, was hellish and blinding. The simultaneous blast of the twelve 18-inch guns rocked the giant ship from side to side. The huge 18-inch anti-aircraft shells exploded just 2,000 feet out from the carrier—and they were absolutely frightening, like little nukes blowing up in space. Add in all the other weapons being fired—SAMs, Bofors twin-barrels, CIWS Gatling guns—and it conjured up a nightmarish scene where nothing could possibly get through such a wall of fire.

Yet something did.

The smoke cleared and those in the war room were stunned to see about two thirds of the drones were still flying. They'd made it through their fusillade somehow, meaning at least a hundred tons of high explosive was still heading for the carrier, more than enough to turn the big boat into a flaming, hulking wreck.

Starr could feel the last moments of someone's life ticking away. He didn't know what to do. The communications guy must have had hundreds of frequencies to go through, and though his hands were still moving at a blur, there just wasn't enough time left to find the right one.

Two things happened next. He remembered seeing the communications guy actually look up for a second, to find his own reflection in the glass of the TV screen along with the slightly distorted image of the crowd of crewmembers behind him, breathlessly watching the drama. But among them he could clearly see Angel. The man seemed puzzled seeing her, maybe because someone dressed casually in jeans and a white baseball cap really stood out on the carrier and especially at this moment.

In that exact instant, the frequency he'd clicked onto started howling with white noise and electronic beeps, with a very robotic-sounding voice trying to be heard above it all.

He'd done it.

He'd found the frequency the enemy used to control its drones. The killer bugs were about twenty seconds away now. The man hastily opened up an audio link and started yelling: "Abort! Abort!"

He hadn't planned for this part because he never thought he'd get this far. "Abort" was the only thing he could think to say.

But it was not enough for the killer drones to break off the attack. But it did do something . . .

The eyes of everyone in the room were fixed on the approaching UAVs, now less than two football fields away. Then in a minute of many surprises, something else completely unexpected happened: the swarm suddenly dropped their bombs. The bombs fell into the sea, many of them exploding on impact.

Those in the war room couldn't believe it. The plan had worked . . . sort of. Whatever their electronic ears had heard from him, the man's commands caused the UAVs to drop their payloads prematurely. But while the drones were no longer carrying any ordnance, they were still heading right for the carrier.

They started slamming into the flight deck seconds later. Even without their bombs, each impact sounded like a stick of dynamite going off. The drones weighed a few hundred pounds each and they still had fuel in their tanks, so when they hit at 120 MPH, it was with a substantial force and caused large explosions.

First there were dozens, and then hundreds. Within seconds, impact blasts were going off up and down the length of the ship. The quarter-mile long flight deck, the skyscraper-like superstructure, the mammoth turrets—nothing was spared. Once again, the mighty ship began rocking violently from side to side.

It seemed to last forever—or at least nearly a minute for all of the 600-plus drones to hit the carrier.

But then, just as suddenly, it was over.

The flight deck was aflame from bow to stern and the wreckage of the drones was piled more than ten feet high in some places, sending out choking clouds of smoke.

But the aircraft carrier was still afloat.

The crowd in the war room broke out in spontaneous cheers and applause; their sense of relief was palpable. Everyone was breathing again, including Starr himself.

He looked at Angel who just smiled back—there but not there.

She was right.

Things were very different here.

Flash!

Suddenly Starr was in the cockpit of a B-52 Stratofortress.

Hawk Hunter was at the controls; his co-pilot's name was Tony, the same man who sat behind the communication console on the aircraft carrier. Two other B-52 Stratofortresses were flying alongside them, all three at 42,000 feet. Through the radio chatter back and forth, Starr came to understand that all three of the giant warplanes were loaded with 70,000 pounds of bombs each in their internal weapons bays, plus crates of dynamite and barrels of gasoline were tied down inside the plane from the navigator's station back to the tail.

And, oh yes, Hunter and Tony were flying all three of them, this one by hand and the other two by communicating via radio with their autopilots.

Angel was beside Starr; again they were there but not there. She didn't have to speak to him at this point. It was obvious he was here to watch and learn how these unusually heroic Americans did things in their battles against Viktor Robotov. In this case, they were over the South Pacific and heading for three islands nearby that boasted units of a huge mercenary army under Viktor's control, the same people who attacked the carrier with drones. The islands were code-named Disney, Death Pit and Battery.

The trio of bombers first approached Disney Island; it had an impressive-sized mountain on its northern side. Viktor's mercenary army operated a huge hangar and a secret base inside this mountain.

The island's extensive SAM network was beginning to burn red hot as could be seen on one of the TV screens on the bomber's control panel. The radio chatter said the three high flying airplanes were only a minute away from being directly over the island.

A barrage of SA-2 SAM missiles was launched at them a moment later. But on Hunter's countdown the three B-52s executed a brilliant last-second fall-away flip maneuver that served to confuse the radar guidance systems of the SAMs while getting the bombers screaming down to an almost impossible altitude. Suddenly the three B-52s were flying at just 1,000 feet, with the SAMs overshooting them by miles and either exploding harmlessly or going wildly off course.

Now the three B-52s came over Disney Island one at a time, in a staggered-line formation. The lead B-52 roared over the island unmolested, quickly disappearing into the morning mist. The second Stratofortress, with Hunter and Tony at the controls was right on its tail.

But at the last instant, the third in line B-52 suddenly veered off course, turned on its left wing, hit the ground and cartwheeled into the side of the island's mountain, exploding like a small atom bomb. It collapsed the northern end of the peak and vaporized the secret base within.

Starr couldn't believe it. These guys used huge bombers as suicide drones?

The two-plane formation flew on, still at barely 1,000 feet. Soon another island came into view. This was the one code-named Death Pit. The enemy soldiers on the island spotted the B-52s and opened up on them, but only with small arms fire. There were no SAM sites on Death Pit Island because as Starr understood it, it was basically a mass grave.

Though a storm of tracer fire rose from the island, it had no effect on the huge bombers. Starr watched as the B-52 in front of him, nose downward, went to full power—and slammed into the side of the island where the enemy forces were concentrated. It hit with such force, it caused such an explosion that a small mushroom cloud rose above the island.

This left just Hunter's Stratofortress—and it was heading for Battery Island.

And at that point, Hunter turned to Tony and said: "Now, comes the fun part . . ."

Because now came the most crucial element of all: the two had to *bail out* of their B-52 as it was just an enormous suicide drone as well. It was clear Tony had been dreading this moment.

He yelled over to Hunter: "It's different for you. You do this kind of stuff all the time!"

To which Hunter replied: "No, I don't. *This* is nuts . . ."

Hunter quickly armed the 70,000 pounds of bombs in the plane's bomb bay, while Tony connected the fuses for the packed HE to a pair of leads on a small car battery.

They were both wearing parachutes, but this was not going to be an ejection. The B-52 threw ejecting pilots out of a stricken craft with such violence, it could affect the speed and more importantly the course of the huge bomber.

So, yes, this was in fact a bail out. They both hurried down to the bottom tier of the jet where Hunter used his boot to kick open the under-fuselage access panel. The first thing they saw of the outside world was an SA-7 portable anti-aircraft missile streaking by not twenty feet away.

Tony looked at Hunter helplessly. The plane was less than 300 feet from plowing in. As calmly as possible, Hunter said to him, "Remember to pull the cord."

Then he pushed Tony through the hole, and he went out right behind him.

Flash!

It took the tiny fleet about thirty minutes to pass by them, but for Starr it seemed like no time at all.

He looked west as the ships slowly disappeared over the horizon.

"You can see these people are not ordinary individuals," Angel told him. "They are doing what you've always tried to do, stop evil wherever it happens, wherever it lives or hides.

"We are in two worlds, two universes, two dimensions, but America is the same here as it is where we are from. The idea that everyone is equal and that as fellow Americans we look out for each other. We help each other, we protect each other. We respect the people who fought and died for us—in either place. We only believe in the truth, even when people we know lie to our faces and try to con us, to grift us. But we're smarter than that. Truth is our greatest weapon. These people believe it and so do we. That's what America is really about. It was great in the first place."

The last of the ships were almost out of sight now.

"If what I fear is true," Angel said after a while. "And Viktor is bouncing back and forth between worlds, we have to help our fellow Americans and defeat him in their world just as much as they can help us defeat him on ours. Right?"

Starr's eyes were still focused on the last ship of the American fleet as it disappeared over the horizon.

"It's the only way to be," he replied.

About the Author

Mack Maloney has written more than 50 novels including the best-selling *Wingman* series and the *Codename:Starman* military mystery series, as well as three nonfiction books, *Mack Maloney's Haunted Universe*, *Beyond Area 51* and *UFOs in Wartime*. Mack is also the host of the nationally syndicated radio show and podcast "Mack Maloney's Military X-Files."

Upcoming New Release!

MACK MALONEY

WINGMAN

Book 23

FASTER THAN FAST

For more information visit: www.SpeakingVolumes.us

On Sale Now!

MACK MALONEY

CODENAME: STARMAN *SERIES*

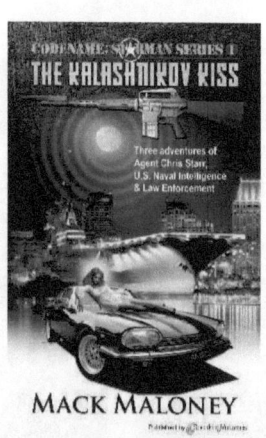

**For more information
visit: www.SpeakingVolumes.us**

Now Available!

ERIC HELM

Sci-Fi Fantasy / Military War

**For more information
visit: www.SpeakingVolumes.us**

www.ingramcontent.com/pod-product-compliance
Lightning Source LLC
LaVergne TN
LVHW041707070526
838199LV00045B/1247